ICE COLD PLAYER

BEYOND THE ICE
BOOK 1

NIKKI HALL

ICE COLD PLAYER

Copyright © **2024 Nikki Hall.** All rights reserved.

No parts of this publication may be reproduced, stored in a retrieval system, or transmitted in any form or by any means, electronic, mechanical, photocopying, recording, or otherwise including AI, without the prior written permission of the copyright owner.

This book is sold subject to the condition that it shall not, by way of trade or otherwise, be lent, resold, hired out, or otherwise circulated without the publisher's prior consent in any form of binding or cover other than that in which it is published and without a similar condition including this condition being imposed on the subsequent purchaser. Under no circumstances may any part of this book be photocopied for resale.

This is a work of fiction. Any similarity between the characters and situations within its pages and places or persons, living or dead, is unintentional and co-incidental.

Cover designed by Angela Haddon

Edited by Megan Clements, Waypoint Author Academy

Thanks for picking up this copy of Ice Cold Player! If you'd like to go back to where everything begins, grab your FREE copy of Game Changer, the prequel novella for the Wild Card series featuring the TU football players and our girl, Eva.

For a FREE copy of Game Changer, go to www.nikkihallbooks.com/signup.

For all the girl bosses out there. Do good in the world, and don't take shit from anyone.

1

Eva

Day one of my senior year in college, and I was homeless. Prospectless. Hopeless. Probably several other -lesses I didn't have the energy to conjure up. After a week of tireless effort, not a single apartment, house, condo, or other would let me move in with my duck.

I didn't want to admit I was giving up, but damn, even my unparalleled manifestation abilities couldn't create an acceptable housing situation out of thin air. There were a million other things going on in my life I should probably be focused on—the coveted assistantship, Juliet the cheer traitor, Dad's new political aspirations, not to mention his dating agreement. Housing, though, was an immediate problem I'd thought I could solve with little effort. A win to start the semester off right.

Yeah, not so much.

Sweat dotted my forehead, and I tilted my face up to the blazing sun, hoping the heat would dry some of the tears. I hated crying, hated letting people see me cry even more, which was why I'd tucked myself away in a little-known courtyard behind the business building. The crumbling concrete fountain in the middle had seen better days and most of the foliage was overgrown with weeds.

Except for the area bordering the edge of campus. Pine trees grew in thick clumps, but the azalea bushes had taken over the ground level in a riot of color. Teagan University had a beautiful campus, but this spot was my favorite.

The faint scent of coffee blew through on a light breeze, compliments of Wildcat Coffee right around the corner, and I could almost imagine this was any other day. If not for the constant texts from my friend group talking about practice and classes.

I silenced my phone and set it next to me. They meant well, but they weren't helping. I returned to my sun worship pose, but my serenity didn't last long. Quiet footsteps marked the approach of an interloper.

A shadow blocked the warmth, and I sighed, accepting I wasn't going to find any more peace today. When I opened my eyes, my heart sank. Standing above me with his arms crossed was my coffee nemesis. Gavin King. Yes, I knew his name, but I refused to use it. 'Hey asshole' worked just as well.

He grunted and took up a position next to my spot on the wall of the fountain. We'd never had a real conversation, so I had no idea what he was doing here popping my solitude bubble.

When I peeked at him from under my lashes, he stared straight ahead at the azaleas, seemingly content to stand there and ruin my afternoon.

"What do you want?" I finally asked.

"You looked upset." He stated it as a fact, and my shoulders tensed up at the thought anyone had noticed.

Out of habit, I went on the offensive. "So you came out here to gloat?"

His lips tipped up on the end, but he didn't take the bait. "No. I came out here to make sure you weren't about to take a header into the fountain."

I glanced at the shallow green water and shuddered. "Gross. Why would you care?"

"Because I'd probably have to clean the fountain after. This is technically part of Wildcat Coffee, and they hate their employees."

I hadn't known my favorite coffee shop owned my favorite piece of land. Like everything else around here, I'd assumed TU owned it.

"Maybe they only hate grumpy employees who've never heard of customer service."

He chuckled, low and slow, and I hated the way the sound shivered up my spine. "I think they're okay with me not handing out free espresso shots to all the girls who smile at me, Princess."

The nickname did it. I couldn't stand assholes who assumed since I was pretty and rich I must be entitled. The stupid sad feelings I hadn't been able to shake were banished with a flash of temper. "I smile at everyone, jackass."

"Not the way you smiled at me." His lazy, confident tone irked me to no end.

Yes, I'd thought he was hot the first time I'd seen him—I wasn't blind—but he'd been surly and rude. I didn't reward that kind of behavior with my good graces. Then he'd proven me right by fucking with one of my friends.

I clawed back the scathing retort he was no doubt expecting, choosing to gift him with my silence instead. Maybe if I ignored him, he'd go away.

His posture shifted as he cast a quick look down at me. "Might as well tell me what's wrong since I'm not going back inside until you do. No reason to prolong the torture."

I hated him and his confidence and his unflappable calm, but my mouth went rogue and blurted out the story of my final appointment of the afternoon. Bob the office manager had laughed in my face when I inquired about a pet deposit for my duck and asked if I meant dick instead. Then he'd offered me a discount if I was nice to him—his words.

Gavin's jaw tensed as I talked, and when I stopped for breath, it took a second for him to unclench enough to talk. "I hope you reported him."

"Oh yeah. I walked out and called the owner immediately. Despite apologizing profusely and promising to fire my good buddy Bob, he couldn't allow a duck as a pet in the complex." I sighed, feeling slightly better now that someone else had reinforced my reaction.

He shook his head slightly. "If your duck is the problem, why not leave it behind?"

My hands clenched in my lap. So much for feeling better. "I'm not abandoning Henry simply because things got hard. I'll find a place. Just probably not today."

He pulled a fuzzy, black, cat ear headband from his back pocket and sat down next to me on the stone lip of the fountain. "I heard you were engaged to that football player. Maybe you could move in with him."

I snorted. "No. Mac and I were involved for a very short time, and now it's over."

His head tilted just enough to meet my gaze. "He didn't meet the royal standards?"

My stomach did a curious flip at the direct eye contact. Gavin was objectively beautiful. Not in a shiny, perfect way, but in a gravelly, rough, fuck me against a brick wall kind of way. Too bad his personality ruined it.

"I don't know why you think I'm going to give you details about my personal life."

"You already did." He lifted one hand to tick off fingers. "I know you don't have a place to stay. I know you're irrationally attached to your duck. I know you have no problem metaphorically throat punching someone. And I know your last relationship ended because of you."

I winced, unable to hide my reaction fast enough. "None of this is your business."

He shrugged. "You're welcome to leave any time."

My hackles rose at the idea of him scaring me away. This was *my* place. He could leave. "And you're welcome to stop being an asshole. Looks like neither of us is going to get what we want."

He scrubbed a hand down his face, and I thought I caught the edge of a grin before he hid it with his fingers. "Whatever you say."

I shifted to face him, trying to decide if I'd rather strangle him or shove him into the fountain. "We didn't have the right chemistry."

"Still sounds like your fault. It's okay. It can be hard to work up a sweat for the peasants."

He was needling me. On purpose. I could see it in the subtle way he watched me as he let his barbs fly. I couldn't figure out if it was because he took joy in kicking someone while they were down or if he was trying to distract me from Bob and his ilk.

Honestly, his motivations didn't matter. Despite knowing what he was doing, I couldn't stop myself from responding.

I leaned in to poke his bicep. "I work up a sweat just fine.

Don't judge my sex life based on your own lackluster efforts."

He turned to fully face me and grinned. "You couldn't handle me, Princess."

I wanted to wipe that smug smile off his face. I wanted to prove I wasn't a poor little rich girl incapable of passion. I wanted to kiss him. The thought shocked me, but I was too far gone to make a good decision.

Quickly, before I could change my mind, I fisted the T-shirt over his chest and closed the distance between us. Gavin didn't miss a beat. His mouth descended on mine as his hand speared through my hair, gripping tight.

Heat rushed through me, stealing my breath and making me tremble. I expected an angry, bruising kiss, but he softened. He explored and teased. I swallowed a whimper and released the clenched fabric to flatten my palm over his racing heart. So it wasn't just me.

Gavin changed the angle, coaxing my lips open. A flurry of what-ifs sped through my mind in rapid succession. What if I climbed into his lap? What if I dropped my hand a little lower? What if I'd been wrong this whole time?

No. Bad decisions happened when I let my lady parts lead the way. I shoved against his chest, and he backed away immediately. For a split second, I saw raw hunger on his face, then it disappeared behind his usual arrogant expression.

I stood and brushed imaginary dirt off my shorts as if I kissed my arch nemesis in a secluded courtyard every day.

"It wasn't me." I turned on my heel and followed the path out of the courtyard, willing my heart rate to return to normal.

2

Gavin

What the fuck was that? I snapped out of my lusty haze in time to sprint after her before she made it much past the fountain.

I didn't know why I bothered chasing her. The kiss was hot, but I had my pick of puck bunnies that *didn't* hate my guts. Eva Adams was everything I avoided in a woman. Spoiled, entitled, high maintenance...

Except she'd been crying.

The self-proclaimed queen of campus had hidden herself away in this trashy little courtyard to cry. Alone.

I caught her wrist and hauled her to a stop. "Wait."

She glared down at my hand on her skin until I let go, but she didn't immediately start running again. "I'm done talking to you."

Irritation warred with the annoying urge to see what she'd do if I kissed her again. Probably stab me with something. Or hire a hit man. Irritation won.

I adopted the smug smile I used to needle her. "I might have a solution for your housing problem." The words surprised me almost as much as they seemed to surprise her. I hadn't intended to offer her a place to live, but it was too late to take them back now.

Her brows rose, then dropped in suspicion. "What kind of solution?"

For a split second, I considered proposing my bed, but even on my worst day, I wasn't that hard up. She'd destroy my life without a second thought. Not to mention she expected me to make the suggestion. I hated being predictable.

"Not that kind, Princess. Get your mind out of the gutter."

I watched her face struggle to maintain composure. Even murderous, she was pretty. Blue eyes the color of ice tried to skewer me as she tucked her pink-streaked hair behind one ear.

She surprised me by not engaging. Instead, Eva took a shallow breath and lifted her chin.

"You have a solution that can accommodate a duck?"

I ran a hand through my short hair, attempting to buy time. I'd forgotten about the damn duck, but her weird pet wasn't the problem. *She* was. Her and my inability to stop myself from making a supremely stupid decision.

"Yes. I live in a house with some of my teammates, and we have an empty room."

She laughed. In my face. Hard. "No. Not even if you had a magic dick that guaranteed multiple orgasms."

Her absolute rejection of my offer made me even more determined to make it work. "My dick isn't part of the deal."

Eva's smile slipped, and she tilted her head. "What *is* the deal?"

"You and your duck can stay in the empty bedroom..." I didn't have an ending to that sentence.

We used the room to hold junk and equipment since the

house lacked a garage or any storage for big stuff. It wouldn't be a problem to make space, but I hated the idea of letting her stay for free. Her attitude made it clear she assumed life would be easy. Case in point, she didn't see how her ridiculous insistence on keeping the duck could end with her homeless.

She raised a brow when I trailed off. "And I agree not to smother you in your sleep? I'm not sure I can make that promise. I can pay."

"I don't want your money."

"What do you want then?"

I let my gaze trail over her. She was tiny. The top of her head barely hit my shoulder, but her personality made her seem bigger. Eva took up space unapologetically, and I was here for it even if she grated on my nerves. Subtle curves hid under her loose tee shirt, and her shorts showed off long, toned legs. I made my way back up to her face, and warning sirens went off in my head as my fingers twitched with the urge to touch her again.

Eva crossed her arms. "If you're imagining me in a French maid costume, enjoy the visual because that's all you'll get."

Like a lightning bolt, an image hit me of Eva on her hands and knees scrubbing the kitchen floor—her tight little ass in the air and her eyes on me. I swallowed a groan and forced myself to focus. The idea wasn't half bad.

I shrugged. "The costume isn't necessary, but whatever makes you feel comfortable."

Her eyes widened slightly, the only sign I'd surprised her. "I'm not playing hide the feather duster with you for a room."

"No, you'll do the cooking and cleaning at the house if you want a room."

"You want me to be the house mom? What is this, the 1950s? Do you even realize how sexist you're being right now?"

"Not sexist. I'd offer the same deal to anyone who wants a room for free." I hadn't considered it before this moment, but as time went on, I liked the idea more and more. My roommates and I were pretty messy during the season, and I didn't need the money from another renter.

She propped her hands on her hips. "I don't want a free room. I want a room I pay for that doesn't include domestic duties."

"Too bad. You're not going to get your way this time, Princess. We take turns cooking and cleaning, but it's a hassle between classes and practice and games. Half the time it doesn't get done and I'm tired of living in a pigsty."

"You live with a bunch of athletes. Seems like a purposeful choice instead of a problem."

My shoulders relaxed at her clear disdain. Eva would never stoop to manual labor. I could chalk this conversation up to temporary insanity caused by seeing the tears staining her cheeks. She wasn't crying now. Mission accomplished.

Instead of storming off, she pulled out her phone. "What's your landlord's information?"

Panic tightened me right back up again, and I refused to acknowledge the tiny kernel of pleasure at her resilience. "Not important. The lease is under my name, and I sublet the bedrooms to the guys. I know the owner, and I guarantee the duck won't be a problem. Take it or leave it."

Her lips pressed together, but she still didn't back down. "Fine. I'll take the room. Since I'm not paying rent, I'll contract a service."

Shit. I couldn't have random people around when Danny could drop by and cause trouble at any time. Besides,

Mase would never let a team of professionals into his space. "No. I want *you* to do it."

Her eyes narrowed. "Excuse me?"

"Three of my teammates live here, and I don't need them distracted by even more people invading our privacy. What's the matter? Too good to be the help?"

"And *I* won't be a distraction?"

She would, but I'd make sure I was the only one affected. "It's a risk I'm willing to take for you."

"You think I'm going to buy that bullshit reason?"

I grinned, sensing a win. "It's not the only reason, Princess. Just the only one I'm willing to share with you. Feel free to keep scouring Addison for duck-friendly places to live. Maybe daddy could buy you a house."

She chewed on her lower lip, and I knew this was my last chance to escape. My feet stayed rooted to the ground. I couldn't imagine the Eva I knew actually accepting my deal, but she hadn't slapped me and stormed out of the courtyard. She stood in front of me, considering the offer.

I told myself to move. Leave her behind and let her solve her own problems. If she agreed, I'd be putting my future at risk. I had one more season to convince Dallas they hadn't wasted their draft on me, and according to Carter McKay, my advisor, they hadn't forgotten the scandal that landed me at TU in the first place.

Eva was exactly the kind of drama I needed to avoid. I should never have stopped her from leaving.

I took a step toward Wildcat Coffee, intending to forget this conversation ever happened, but Eva let out a frustrated growl.

"I'll take the room in exchange for the cooking and half the cleaning. I have classes and practice too. My cooking skills are nonexistent, so you'll have to deal with a meal service unless you want food poisoning."

Fuck. She wasn't supposed to make a counteroffer. "No deal. I'll accept a meal service, but you do *all* the cleaning."

"I want an itemized list of what I have to clean, approved by both of us, and I want to meet the other roommates first. How many are there?"

I faced her again, trapped by my own instincts. "Three other guys. Mason Black, Reece Tanner, and Cole Mathis."

They'd be ecstatic I found us someone to take care of the house, especially someone who looked like her. I imagined Reece wouldn't last a day without making a play. He'd never met a woman he couldn't charm. Mase would probably ignore her, and Cole would become her new best friend.

As if she could hear my thoughts, she perked up at Cole's name. "At least you have good taste in friends."

The thought of Eva and Cole hooking up tied my insides into knots, and an irrational burst of anger burned away my survival instincts.

"Deal's off if you fuck any of my roommates."

She tossed her hair over her shoulder. "You don't get any say in my sex life."

I stepped forward, invading her space, and she met me toe to toe. Her chin tilted up with stubborn determination, daring me to push her just a little more.

"If you're that hard up, you can always pay a different way." I'd never used sex for barter before, but Eva's constant defiance activated some hidden caveman part of me. She was dangerous, yet I couldn't stop myself from seeing how close I could get. I leaned into the feral attraction, letting my gaze linger on her lips, a reminder of the scorching kiss she'd laid on me not fifteen minutes ago.

A hitch in her breath, barely noticeable but there, increased the tension between us. The air thickened, heavy in my chest as I fought to remember why I disliked her. Eva broke first, tossing me a reprieve with her sassy fucking mouth.

"Your roommates are off limits, but you're not? Classy. Also, I don't fuck people I live with. Too messy." She shoved her phone against my chest, somehow using the motion to create space between us. The girl was strong. "Text yourself, then you can send the address and an itemized chore list. When do I move in?"

"What about meeting the other guys?"

"I trust Cole."

But not me. The implication was clear with the soft way she said his name. In the last two years of living with Cole, I'd never once been jealous of him until now. He was the nicest guy on the planet, and I'd happily toss him into traffic if I caught him with Eva.

I told myself the possessive streak heating my blood was rooted in keeping my friends free of Eva's influence, but the drama was already starting. Everything about this was a horrible idea. I should channel the asshole persona she'd assigned me on our first meeting and tell her nevermind. I should turn and walk away without digging myself any deeper.

I should definitely not kiss her again.

Eva's lips parted, and I reached up to wrap my fingers around her phone. "Why not today? We have a late practice, but you can come by anytime. Reece always leaves the door unlocked."

I broke the connection to send myself a text. She could ruin me—discover my secrets and use them against me, destroy my friendships—all with a sweet smile, but the animosity and trouble weren't enough to push me past one simple fact.

She'd been crying alone in a broken courtyard.

The afternoon sun passed behind the business building as I handed her phone back, stretching the shadows out to touch the fountain. Eva tucked the phone into her shorts pocket then held out a hand.

I stared down at her slim fingers for a long beat before sliding my palm against hers. "This isn't a truce."

"I know," she replied quietly. "It's a deal with the devil."

3

Eva

"Don't look at me like that, Henry. You know it's for the best." Five hours and forty-seven minutes had passed since I'd agreed to Gavin's deal. Not that I was counting.

I'd spent the past two nights crashing on Lizzy's bedroom floor in her sorority house. My back was killing me, Henry was acting out since Lizzy didn't have her own bathroom, and I'd do some sketchy shit for a full fat latte.

The second Gavin had left the courtyard, I'd called my movers to get my bedroom furniture out of storage. I didn't know the situation at his house, but if the room came furnished, I'd happily foot the bill for storing whatever mismatched IKEA disaster the guys had collected.

My inner circle consisted entirely of football players and their girlfriends. Experience dictated athletes didn't pay much attention to their living arrangements as long as the food was plentiful. A tiny pang twisted my heart at the thought of them doing movie nights without me, but it had been my idea to leave—as misguided as it probably was.

By this point, my expectations couldn't get any lower.

Henry gave me a disgruntled quack from her crate on the passenger seat, and I turned off the engine. She didn't like being cooped up, but I refused to drive with a loose duck in the car.

For the third time, I checked the address Gavin had texted earlier. The numbers on the house were correct, but I couldn't wrap my mind around four hockey players living in a cute two-story on a quiet street in Addison's version of the suburbs.

Sunset had passed a while ago, so streetlights lit up the neighborhood. A bushy tree blocked part of the upper level from my view, and bushes lined the front under a big picture window. The houses on either side glowed with warm light, but Gavin's windows were dark.

Everything looked so...normal. Like I expected a couple of kids to be playing in the yard.

My parents would love it, especially now that Dad had decided being rich wasn't enough, he needed to get into politics too. They didn't know about the duck problem, and if I had my way, they'd never find out. Bad enough they'd cornered me into letting them set me up with some respectable dates the next couple of months.

As far as they were concerned, I wasn't using my time at college appropriately to find a husband. Dad was willing to wait me out until his campaign advisor found an old pic of me and Mac. He didn't approve of my dating choices, and he approved even less when he found out we hadn't actually been dating.

There was nothing wrong with not wanting a serious relationship to go with my orgasms. Dad disagreed on the grounds I was presenting the wrong kind of image. The message wasn't new—I'd never been a good enough replacement for my brother—but the threat to pull my funding got my attention. At least he hadn't demanded I actually marry one of them. A couple of dates I could handle.

As cute as this house was, Dad would absolutely hate the four roommates. I scooped Henry out of her crate and held her in my lap. My stomach twisted into knots as I imagined all the worst-case scenarios stemming from my spiral into madness earlier.

Henry wiggled her warm little body closer, and I stroked her soft feathers. We'd parked across from the house to wait for the movers, but I had trouble making myself get out of the car. The free fall of panic I'd been ignoring for the last week was still lurking under the surface. Thanks to my reckless actions this afternoon, I could add in dread. Gavin's mouth was one hundred percent off limits, but my common sense didn't stop me from reliving the kiss every time I let my guard down.

Hopefully, proximity to Gavin's shitty attitude would cure me of any lingering curiosity about the rest of his skills. If nothing else, I could find a suitable hookup to relieve the pressure. Though I'd have to be careful about who I brought home considering my new roommates.

On cue, a nondescript older sedan rolled down the street and pulled into the driveway. All four doors opened, and a group of guys piled out. They gathered around the trunk to pull out duffel bags and sticks. With the windows open, I could hear them clearly. Two of the big guys shoved back and forth trying to reach into the back at the same time, and the driver laughed.

Even in the dark, I recognized Gavin—his gravelly chuckle raised goosebumps across my skin. The other three must be his roommates. Judging by their sweaty clothes and the faint stink wafting my direction on the breeze, they'd just come from practice. Not so different from football players actually.

Maybe this could work.

My momentary confidence was ruined when Henry waddled over to the open window and quacked loudly at the shenanigans. Gavin's eyes shot to mine, finding me unerringly before I could back deeper into the shadows.

Not that I would. Eva Adams hid from no man.

I straightened my shoulders, lifted my chin, and mercilessly shoved the unease into the farthest corner of my mind. The guy standing next to Gavin followed his gaze, and I glanced at him, surprised to realize I hadn't recognized Cole, who I actually liked.

Granted, I hadn't seen him in months, not since my birthday at the beginning of the year. He'd cut his hair. The shaggy length used to hang all over the place, but now it was short on the sides and slightly longer on top where it stuck up in tiny spikes. The look suited the sharp planes of his face, and I'd bet he got a lot more attention from the ladies now.

Cole was hot. Not Gavin level hot, but close. I took quick stock of the others and groaned. All four of them were attractive. Lean, muscled, broad shouldered, I was surprised there weren't ball bunnies camped out on the lawn.

Wait, hockey groupies weren't ball bunnies. Puck bunnies? Shit, I needed to learn the language before I ended up being the morning after bunny remover.

Gavin stepped forward under the streetlight and smirked at Henry in the window. "You going to introduce us, Princess?"

Cole snorted out a laugh then quickly smothered it when I glowered at him. He held out his hands in a peace gesture. "If you'd called me, I'd have let you pay rent like a normal person."

Gavin elbowed him in the gut, and Cole let out an *oof* as he doubled over. "Stay out of it, Mathis."

The other two ambled our way, and I finally exited the car, circling to stand next to Henry's window in case she got any ideas about her ability to fly. As a duck, she *could* fly—she just preferred to be carried. Which meant she was more the falling with style type.

Gavin nodded his head at me. "This is Eva, the one I told you about."

I frowned at the silent message that passed between them. "Nice to meet you."

The tallest one with piercing green eyes and tousled dark blond hair grinned at me. "Welcome home, beautiful."

Gavin rolled his eyes. "That one's Reece Tanner, shameless flirt. The other is Mason Black. He's our goalie, and I have no idea what goes through his head on any given day."

Mason gave me a sharp smile and a salute. Like Gavin, he had tattoos on his arms, but his snaked all the way down his hands. "I'm grabbing a shower."

He turned and left without another word, snagging his bag and sticks on the way into the house. When I sent Gavin a questioning look, he shrugged.

"Not everyone warmed to the idea right away."

Cole shook his head. "Mase can be an asshole, but he'll get over it. Need me to carry anything?"

I shook my head, staring up the empty street. "I don't have much in the car. My movers have the rest of my stuff in the truck."

Gavin frowned. "How long have you been waiting?"

I checked my watch, surprised by the time. "About a half hour."

"What time were they supposed to arrive?"

"They were supposed to beat us here." I felt stupid for letting myself get so distracted by my new digs I didn't notice something was wrong with the movers. With a sigh, I pulled up the number for the company and went over the terms of the contract in my head. They'd charged extra for the after-hours move, but they'd promised immediate service.

After five rings, their voicemail informed me I could leave a message or call back during business hours. I had a message for them, but it wasn't appropriate for little duck ears. My lips pressed together as I jabbed at the end button.

Gavin held out his hand.

I raised a brow. "Yes?"

"Let me try."

My fingers tightened around the phone. "They didn't answer. You being in possession of a penis does not make companies magically pick up the phone."

He wiggled his fingers and Cole snickered, so I slapped the phone into his hand. His lips twitched as he put the call on speaker.

I opened my mouth to mock him again, and a gruff voice answered the call.

"'Lo?"

"Hey, my friend—" I snorted loudly at the description, and Gavin turned his back on me without missing a beat. "Eva Adams hired you guys tonight to move her, but her truck hasn't arrived yet."

"One second." The loud clacking of a keyboard filled the quiet. "Adams? Says here they arrived to the pickup on time, but the truck got a flat on the way to the dropoff. Delivery is delayed until tomorrow."

"Were you planning to tell her that?"

A chair squeaked in the background. "We operate with a twenty-four hour delivery window, tomorrow morning is still within the window. Need anything else?"

Gavin turned to raise his brow at me, and I couldn't do anything but shake my head, cursing the fine print on the contract I clearly hadn't read closely enough.

"No, that's all. Thank you." Gavin's polite response added a level of irrational anger to the frustration already spiking my blood pressure.

The guy grunted and hung up.

Reece clapped Gavin on the back and offered me a grin. "Problem solved. Since my muscles are no longer needed, I'm going to raid the fridge." He jerked his chin at Cole. "You coming?"

Another one of those annoying messages passed between Cole and Gavin, then Cole shrugged. "Yeah, I could eat."

Part of me wanted Cole to stay and act as a buffer, but the bigger part—the one licking her lips at the chance to lay into Gavin without witnesses—gave him a finger wave when his gaze shifted to me.

"You want something to eat, Eva?"

"I'm good, but can you take Henry inside please? She's been cooped up all day."

His brows shot up when I pointed to Henry's little brown face peeking out next to me, but I didn't give him a chance to say no. Henry chattered at me when I hauled her through the open window, and she swung her head to stare at Cole when I unceremoniously shoved her at his chest. As I'd known he would, Cole immediately grabbed my duck with both hands.

I wasn't worried. Cole wouldn't drop her, and Henry

wouldn't make a fuss. She loved being held. I'd run her a bath when I got inside.

"You can put her in my room. Just make sure she can't get to any wires. We're working on her impulse control, and her impulse seems to be to eat anything vaguely worm-shaped."

Reece held up his phone to snap a pic. "This is going on my locker."

Cole flipped him off around his handful of duck and started up the driveway. "Get the door, asshole."

Gavin had stayed quiet through the whole exchange, but I hadn't forgotten about him. He watched me with amused eyes, and the urge to vent all my frustrations from the last week became a physical ache. The pressure built in my chest, crawling up my throat, until I had to swallow a few times to talk.

For Henry's sake, I tried to pretend he was anyone else besides Gavin. "Thank you for speaking to the moving company." *Even though I didn't ask you to, and all you did was exactly what I'd just done.*

I didn't say the words, but when he narrowed his eyes, I was pretty sure he read them in my expression. Gavin held out my phone, and I plucked it from his hand.

He shook his head, wincing at the house. "There's no furniture in your room right now."

His tone wasn't quite as acerbic as mine, but I heard the frustration. Welcome to the club, buddy. "It's not the first time I've slept on the floor. I have a blanket in my car."

Gavin's brow furrowed. "Cole's going to hate the idea."

I shrugged as I grabbed my blanket and purse, then locked up. "Cole's a big boy. He'll get over it. Can you show me which room is mine? It's been a long day, and I'm tired."

The situation wasn't ideal, but I could easily beg

someone for a couch for one more night. I was tired of being transient though. A bare floor in my own room was better than someone else's.

He glanced toward the door then sighed. "You can have my bed. For tonight only. This isn't an invitation."

I frowned, trying to spot the caveat. "Why?"

His hands dove deep into his pockets. "Because you may annoy me to no end, but my mom would murder me from beyond the grave if I let a poor, homeless, duck mom sleep on the floor in an empty room."

The casual mention of his apparently dead mother shut me up real fast. My parents were alive and well, but I was intimately familiar with grief. I blamed the rush of sympathy for my quick capitulation. That and my sore back. I had practice tomorrow, and a good night's sleep would be a blessing with Juliet trying to take over the squad.

"Fine. Show me to *your* room."

"So gracious," he muttered, but he'd already hefted his gear and started toward the house.

I let it go in favor of watching him saunter up the driveway. He had the loose-limbed walk of an athlete who knew his body—filled with confidence that sent a flutter through my lady parts. Broad shoulders tapered to a trim waist, and damn, his ass looked good in those sweats.

He looked over his shoulder, and my eyes shot up to his. Busted. I refused to be embarrassed about appreciating the human form. Gavin's lips curled up a tiny bit, and he held the door open for me.

"Turnabout is fair play, you know."

I raised my chin as I walked past him into the brightly lit living room. "As if anyone could keep their eyes off my ass."

He chuckled behind me, a dark, dangerous sound. "Careful what you wish for, Princess."

4

Eva

I probably shouldn't have taunted my new landlord, but I couldn't help myself. Gavin activated all my instincts to hit first and ask questions later.

The door closed behind us with a quiet click, and Gavin veered around me headed toward the sliding glass door on the other side of the kitchen. I caught a whiff of the most horrible smell imaginable, a cross between rotting socks and a couch left in the rain for a few years.

Dear god, what was in his bag?

I dropped my stuff to pinch my nose closed, blinking until my watering eyes cleared. "What the hell was that?"

Gavin glanced over his shoulder, shoving the slider open. "I thought you spent all your time with athletes?"

"Yeah, but none of them could clear a room with the stink of their gear alone."

He raised a brow as he set the bag outside and closed the door, thankfully trapping the smell on the other side of the glass. "Sounds like they need to work harder then."

I *would not* take offense. I would raise my chin and be the better person. I would—

"Maybe your fiancé should spend less time primping and more time working up a sweat." Gavin tossed me a smug smile, and rage disintegrated any semblance of nice Eva.

"Listen, you puck-addled asshole. You and your hockey buddies wouldn't last a day on the football field. Hell, you wouldn't last a day in my cheer squad. Not that I'd trust you with something as complicated as stunt work. At least Mac knows the difference between skill and brute force."

His smirk didn't falter as he snorted out a disbelieving laugh and turned his back on me to open the refrigerator. "Sure, Princess. Jaden beat your fiancé in a head-to-head footrace, and he's not even the fastest guy on my team."

I growled, shoving the fridge door closed and planting myself in front of it. "They were racing naked and barefoot on a gravel road."

Gavin stared down at me, not bothering to back up despite mere inches separating us. "I truly couldn't care less."

My jaw clenched. "You brought it up."

"And you can't handle a little teasing."

Cole walked into the living room with his hockey bag slung over his shoulder, and the stink—somehow worse than Gavin's—reached me well before the man. I grimaced before I could stop myself.

"I can't live here with that putrid smell," I muttered.

He cast a quick, confused glance between Gavin and I, then made a beeline for the door. "That's why we keep the bags outside."

I sighed, utterly done with the day, and slid away from Gavin. His gaze burned into me, but I ignored him. I was holding on to my sanity by the tattered ends. All I wanted was to go to bed and try again tomorrow. Even if it was the bed of the enemy.

"Where's my duck, Cole?"

"I can handle duck duty tonight. We're vibing, don't worry."

"Henry needs her bath."

Cole flashed me a grin. "I'm an expert at giving a lady a bath."

I leaned sideways to peer around him, searching the stairs for signs of a duck in distress. "She's kind of temperamental."

"Like her owner," Gavin grumbled.

"Exactly." I skewered him with a pointed look. "We both like things a certain way."

Cole backed toward the stairs with a half-smile I didn't trust in the least. "I got this. We used to have ducks on my grandpa's farm."

I resisted the urge to roll my eyes. Naturally, the wholesome hockey player with the heart of gold had spent time on *his grandpa's farm*, probably nursing sick animals back to health or something equally Hallmark worthy. Why couldn't I be attracted to Cole?

Gavin grunted behind me, close, and goosebumps rose in a wave across my skin. Fatigue weighed me down, and I wondered if the guys could see the strain in my muscles from holding myself upright. I hoped not.

Instead of slowly melting into a puddle on the floor, I fixed Cole with my best helpless girl stare—the one with big eyes and even bigger guilt. "I'm trusting you to keep her safe. Don't let me down."

His smile edged closer to genuine. "She's going to be fine. Get some rest, Eva."

Cole bounded up the stairs, and I took half a second to feel sorry for myself before I turned to face Gavin.

"I know I'm supposed to do the food stuff, but can we start tomorrow? I've had a shit day."

He rubbed his chin and nodded slowly. "We already ate on the way home anyway."

I knew it wasn't late by college standards, but I felt like I hadn't slept all week. "If you can show me to your room, I'll get out of the way of whatever a bunch of hockey players do after practice."

He shook his head with a laugh. "I don't know what you're expecting, but we're usually wiped after practice."

I shrugged. "I try not to presume."

"Unless you're talking shit about hockey?" He held up a hand when my mouth dropped open. "Doesn't matter. My room's this way."

Gavin nodded to the first door on the right as we hit the second floor. "That's Cole's room, the one past it is Reece's. You and I are on the other side. Mase's in the basement."

He opened the first door on the left and waved for me to go in ahead of him. I'd expected a mess with half-naked women plastered all over his walls, sports paraphernalia on every surface, and maybe a voodoo doll of me for good measure.

His room was clean, with sparse furniture consisting of a desk, a dresser, and a big ass bed. I was right about the sports stuff. A hockey stick leaned into the corner, and a couple of trophies sat next to a squishy puck on his desk. The jury was still out on the voodoo doll. No naked women on the wall, but three canvas pictures hung over his bed.

A series of artsy photos of a hockey player mid-action, kicking up ice as he chased a puck. I had to admit, they looked good. Moody as hell with the dark background and the light reflecting off the snow. Something about the player looked familiar despite not showing his face, and I could feel the intensity in his coiled muscles—the command of his body. *This* was an athlete.

Gavin nudged me as he walked past, breaking my weird trance. "Do you need something to sleep in?"

I shook my head. "I can sleep in this."

The bed wasn't really made, more like he'd haphazardly tossed the bedding in place after he got up. I sat on the soft mattress and gingerly lifted the blanket to my nose for a sniff test. To my surprise, the bedding smelled good—like dryer sheets and Gavin. I frowned as the thought crossed my mind. I hadn't realized I'd established a "Gavin" scent, nor that I apparently liked it.

I shoved the problematic association to the back of my mind and crawled between the sheets. Gavin didn't say anything else as he emptied his pockets on the desk. The polite part of me instilled by my parents insisted I thank him, or at least tell him goodnight, but I'd spent a lifetime quietly rebelling against my parents' lessons. I rolled to the middle of the bed, pulled the bedspread up to my chin—taking another quick sniff—and waited for Gavin to vacate the room.

Instead of leaving, he reached behind his back and pulled his shirt over his head.

I popped up to a sitting position, letting the blankets gather around my waist. "What are you doing?"

He tossed the shirt toward one of the two closed doors. "Getting ready for bed."

"In here?" My voice squeaked into a new octave.

He opened his arms, encompassing the space. "This *is* my bedroom."

"You said I could sleep in here." My shock was quickly morphing into the suspicion I'd been played.

"Yeah, so scoot over."

No. Absolutely not. I refused to share a bed with my archnemesis knowing I liked the way he smelled. "No. Go sleep on the couch."

"I'm not sleeping on the couch, and neither are you."

"You don't get a say in what I do." I took a deep breath and threw the covers back to stand up. "I'm sorry I gave you the impression I'm a pushover. I'm *really* not."

Gavin caught my elbow, hauling me to a stop, then dropped his hand as if he'd been burned. "Stop being a selfish brat for five seconds and listen."

His big body blocked the door, so I crossed my arms, tilted my head, and waited for his bullshit.

"When Mase can't sleep, he takes over the couch and plays video games all night. We have an unspoken rule to leave the space for him when he needs it. My bed is big enough for both of us to stretch out without touching each other." He raised a brow. "Unless you can't keep your hands to yourself."

My lips pressed together in an effort to keep my violent thoughts inside. I didn't want to alienate my roommates any more than necessary on the first night, and I didn't want to give in to Gavin's taunting. His challenge shouldn't work on me, but dammit, he'd nailed the fear at the heart of my refusal.

I wasn't sure I *could* keep my hands to myself. Mase was enough to get me to stay, but I couldn't let him know he'd hit truth with the other reason.

With a sweet smile, I sauntered past him toward the door. "Since you're concerned, I'll go see if Cole has space. Or Reece. He seems like he'd have a nice big bed." I barely got the words out before Gavin slapped a palm against his door, holding it closed.

"My bed or no one's, Princess." A growl replaced the teasing in his voice.

I pushed against his chest, but he didn't move an inch. "Why do you care?"

"Because I don't want you fucking with their heads."

The way you fuck with mine. He didn't say the words, but I could see them written across his face. At least I wasn't the only one. A tiny zip of satisfaction raced through me, enough to help me claw back some control.

My fingertips burned where they rested on his skin, but I kept my eyes locked on his, ignoring the urge to explore the dark strokes of his tattoo. I'd seen plenty of naked chests in my life without making stupid decisions—this one didn't have to be any different.

I hated capitulating, but I *really* didn't want to sleep on the floor again. "Fine. You can stay."

Gavin's lips tipped up as I broke the staring contest. His arm dropped when I slid away to crawl back into the bed, but he stayed there facing the door for a long moment. I hoped he was reconsidering his stupid demands.

His shoulders rose and fell with a deep breath, then the light snapped off. In the dark, I could barely make out his shadow as he circled the room. I curled up on my side, facing away from him.

The quiet thump of clothes hitting the floor made my back tense up. I clenched my eyes closed, willing my breathing to stay even despite the sudden rush of my pulse. The mattress groaned under his weight, and the blankets pulled taut for a second. My imagination was having a field day trying to decide if he slept in his undies or went commando.

Heat licked at my core, and I squeezed my legs together. No way. I was *not* getting hot and bothered by the thought of Gavin sprawled out naked behind me. I simply hadn't been with a guy since Mac at the end of spring semester, and my body didn't give a fuck who was rustling around under the covers.

Gavin sighed, and his warm breath hit my shoulder, sending goosebumps rippling down my arms and back. A montage of all the times we'd sparred with each other flashed across my mind, ending with the hot as fuck kiss earlier.

Fine. I knew exactly who was taking up all the space behind me. Gavin's body may have been made for dirty fantasies, but I couldn't forget what he'd done to Kayleigh. He was a selfish asshole through and through. One I couldn't stop thinking about.

At this rate, the floor would have been better. At least I would have gotten some sleep.

"Relax, Princess. I won't bite unless you ask nicely." His husky voice broke the heavy silence.

I wanted to pretend I was asleep, but my faking game was weak. "I hate that nickname. I'm no princess."

"No? You seem pretty haughty from where I'm lying."

"If we're going with medieval titles, I'd prefer spymaster... and you'd be the dirty thief trying to gain access to the castle."

He scooted closer, his warmth invading my space. "You're right about one thing..." His lips brushed the shell of my ear, and I couldn't contain the shiver. "I can be very dirty."

With careful effort, I managed to keep my breathing even. I knew he didn't mean what he was implying. He was trying to get a rise out of me in the only way he knew how.

My own fault for giving him ammunition. I never should have kissed him.

When I didn't respond, Gavin's voice lowered. "Are you going to give me access, Princess?"

I closed my eyes for a brief second—steeling myself against the temptation of surrender—then rolled over and smacked him in the face with the blankets. "Not today, Satan. Now move back and toss me those extra pillows."

His lips twitched as he retreated to the far side. "Why?"

"Because I need at least two for the wall between us, one for my head, and one to smother you with."

Instead of handing me a future weapon, he shoved one of his pillows against my belly. "Good enough?"

I huffed and shifted around until I was comfortable, well away from Gavin's reach. "It'll do."

He tucked his arms under his head, staring at the ceiling. "Not even a thank you, huh?"

"I hate you," I said sweetly.

"I hate you too, Princess. Now go to sleep."

5

Gavin

I'd started calling Eva "Princess" in my head the first time we met. Ice queen wasn't quite right with the heat between us the second her eyes hit mine, but she sure as hell frosted me out when I didn't fall for her charms. Too bad for her I liked the ice.

She was anything but cold first thing in the morning.

I woke before my alarm, as usual, but unlike every other morning I got up to hit the rink, I wasn't in a hurry to leave the warmth of my bed. At some point in the night, Eva had burrowed past her pillow wall to curl up next to me.

Her ass snuggled against my morning wood, and my hand rested on the bare skin of her stomach where her shirt had ridden up. Her spicy vanilla scent invaded my head, and I sucked in a deep breath before I could stop myself.

Snickerdoodles. She smelled like the cookies my mom used to bake for me and my brother. Before.

The reminder of Danny hit me like ice water to the dick. I had enough issues without Eva and her first world problems. She'd take advantage of every weakness to get her way, and I couldn't afford for her to use my secrets against me.

Careful not to wake her, I slid away in the pale dawn light and shut myself in the bathroom. I could have claimed the master since my name was on the paperwork, but Reece had begged me for the larger room. The Jack and Jill bathroom was fine for me since I didn't need anything beyond a sink, a toilet, and a place to shower.

I frowned at the door across from mine. Eva's room connected to this bathroom too. My dick twitched with the thought of Eva in here showering, hot water running down her tight little body. Fuck. I really didn't think this through.

I hadn't thought of how close she'd be when I made the offer. For a fleeting moment, I considered tidying up, but fuck that. Eva could deal with the less than pristine bathroom. It was her job now anyway.

Better yet, she could go use the one in the hallway.

With more force than necessary, I wrenched the shower on. Normally, I'd wait until after our morning workout and use the facility, but Eva's spicy vanilla scent followed me into the bathroom. My dick refused to calm the fuck down when I could still feel Eva's soft skin under my hand.

I kicked the boxer-briefs I'd worn last night into the corner and stepped under the spray. Hockey. I needed to focus on hockey. One more year, one more chance to prove myself to Dallas. Danny didn't want to come with me, so he'd be on his own for the first time. Maybe he'd finally get his head out of his ass and grow up.

My eyes flicked in the direction of Eva's bedroom. She could ruin everything if I let my guard down. On cue, my cock hardened as if Eva had walked in here and sunk to her knees with a smile. I rolled my eyes and stroked myself once, twice.

Why her? I could have my pick of puck bunnies. The hockey team may not have the exposure of the football program, but we were making a name for ourselves. Though not among the cheerleaders apparently.

I remembered the glint in Eva's eyes as she insulted us. What did it say about me that the challenge heated my blood?

Nothing good. Probably that I should forgo my usual hands-off policy during the season and find an alternative. Except the idea of a random hookup did nothing for me. I didn't want a generic puck bunny. I wanted a bratty, manipulative cheerleader with pink hair and soft skin.

My eyes closed as I leaned forward to brace myself against the tile wall. We didn't have locks on these bathroom doors, so there was a slight chance Eva could catch me jerking it in the shower. The possibility made me so hard I ached.

Images flashed in my mind, fast and furious. Eva stripping off those little shorts she'd worn to bed. Smirking at me with her sassy fucking mouth. Hopping onto the counter and spreading her pretty thighs. Would she taste as good as she smelled?

The orgasm hit me hard, and I groaned, not caring if she heard me. Day one, and I hadn't even eaten breakfast before I was making bad decisions. Fantasizing about Eva was a slippery slope, especially after last night. She needed to be firmly in the no fucking category. As I finished my shower, I reminded myself she'd had no problem spreading her ridiculous grudge against me to anyone who would listen.

With a towel wrapped around my waist, I gingerly opened the door to the bedroom. While I tried to wipe her from my mind, Eva had taken over the center of my bed. She curled around my pillow, hair splayed across my sheets, and one tanned leg stuck out of the covers.

The urge to climb into bed next to her tightened my

fingers on the towel. I should wake her up. Get her out of my space. My gaze lingered on her toned thigh for a long second, then I turned away. Deliberately keeping my eyes focused elsewhere as I gathered my workout gear.

She'd be gone by the time I got back, and I could go back to ignoring her.

The hallway was quiet, which meant either the others weren't up or they were already gone. The kitchen smelled faintly like bacon and a pan sat in the sink. Yeah, they were already gone. I wasn't late, but I was cutting it closer than usual. The assholes hadn't even tried to wake me up.

The front door opened as I pulled ingredients out of the fridge for a protein shake. I expected Reece to come in and give me shit for making them wait, but the sight of Danny walking through the living room stopped me short.

"What are you doing here?" I grimaced, but I wasn't firing on all cylinders just yet.

He smirked. "Is that any way to greet your twin?"

"For you, yes." I shut the fridge with a clatter and dumped everything into the blender. "What do you want?"

Danny dropped into one of the chairs around our tiny dining room table, stretching his long legs out in front of him. He wore jeans and a plain black shirt that showed off the tattoos inked down his arms. Every time I caught sight of the designs mirroring my own, I had to swallow the urge to lecture him.

He leaned back and crossed his arms behind his head, seemingly oblivious to my shitty mood. "I need a favor."

I snorted quietly. He always needed a favor. "What is it?"

"I have a test in Econ next week. You took that class last year, right?"

"I did," I said slowly.

"I could use a stand in."

"That all?"

"I'm also out of cash."

I tilted my head back to stare at the ceiling. "How are you always out of money? You're the one with a job."

Danny didn't answer right away, and when I dropped my gaze back to him, he pinned me with a sharp smile. "Not all of us got a fancy scholarship, bro."

My hands were busy holding onto the blender, so I settled for a verbal smack down. "Fuck you, man. You had your chance, and you decided you'd rather throw your future—and mine— down the toilet."

"You seem to have recovered just fine from where I'm sitting. I hear TU is going to the Frozen Four this year."

I didn't miss the edge to his tone, but I'd had years of practice ignoring his attempts to bait me. Keeping Danny out of trouble on top of my other responsibilities was exhausting without getting into a shouting match every time I saw him. He wanted to lash out, and I wanted to keep his focus firmly on me where I knew he'd be safe.

He sent me a sly look. "Unless you're too busy with your new roommate."

My gaze jerked to his, meeting the same brown eyes I saw every day in the mirror. "How'd you hear about that?"

He shrugged. "People talk. Especially Reece. He was in the workout room earlier telling one of the puck bunnies how he had a new roomie."

I forced my tense muscles to relax. "I told you to stop using the hockey facility. You have a perfectly good gym on the other side of campus."

"Your machines always work, and the sauna is top notch. Not to mention you share the space with the cheerleaders."

TU's hockey facility was brand new, an attempt to lure top talent away from colder climates, but they'd demolished the previous small athletic weight room to do it. Technically, we had our own weight room, but unlike the football team, Coach Dalton let the other sport programs have access. Most just used the student center, but some of the cheerleaders and a few of the soccer team preferred our set up.

"You're supposed to be keeping a low profile," I reminded him.

"No one knows it's me. I'm careful not to show up when you're there. Now, when were you going to tell me you were living with the campus queen?"

"Ideally, never."

His grin turned feral. "Ooo, possessive. Is she up there in the spare room now?"

"No." I managed to keep my face impassive, but it didn't matter. Danny could read me in the dark.

He leaned forward. "Wait, is she in *your* room? Can I go see?"

I glared at him, but he didn't make any move to sprint up the stairs. "She's sleeping, jackass."

"Daaamn. One night here and you already tired her out."

My smoothie finished blending, and I poured it in a to-go cup. "It's not like that. Her furniture won't be here until today, so I let her use my bed." I was strangely reluctant to share the details with my brother.

He eyed my phone as I pulled it out to send him the money. "You got dibs?"

"I have no interest in Eva. If you like having your balls handed to you, feel free to try." The words tasted sour in my mouth, but I refused to let him think she meant anything to me.

She didn't.

After the transfer went through, I shoved my phone into my pocket and jerked my head at the door. "I have to get to practice."

"I'm happy to stay and make sure your new roomie feels welcome."

I scowled at him. "Out."

Danny raised his hands in surrender and stood. "Fine. I have a shift anyway. About that econ test..."

"Text me the details. If it doesn't get in the way of practice, I'll do it."

I'd learned to pick my battles years ago, and showing up for a test I could probably pass in my sleep wasn't worth a fight. Danny glanced at the stairs one last time as I ushered him out the front door.

He didn't say goodbye—or thanks—as he cut through the grass to his motorcycle parked by the road. I didn't mind helping him out with money, but it grated on my nerves that he refused to take responsibility for his own life. Mom and Dad left us each a pretty hefty inheritance when they died, but Danny blew through his in the first year.

He revved the motorcycle, then took off down the street with a loud, high-pitched whine. Luckily, most of my neighbors should already be at work, but it was yet another example of Danny making himself as obnoxious as possible. At least he wore a helmet.

I locked the door and almost made it into my car before I remembered I'd left my gear on the back porch last night. With a groan, I circled the house through the gate instead of going back inside. On the off-chance Danny had woken up Eva, I didn't want another visual of her long, toned legs.

A prickle of unease skated down my back when I remembered Danny's last lingering look, but even he had to be smart enough not to get involved with Eva. She was infamous for knowing *everything*, and no matter how reckless he'd become, he knew our secrets would hurt him as much as they'd hurt me.

6

Eva

I needed coffee. Thanks to Gavin and his stupid ultimatum, I'd slept better than I had in months, but I didn't have time to wake up slowly. Stephen Delucca waited for no man—or woman—and I desperately needed to FaceTime with my bestie before showing up for cheer practice with Juliet.

Coach Kat—Ekaterina Tucker, but she insisted we call her Kat—was well aware of my extra training over the summer. It hadn't stopped her from appointing a new squad leader in my absence though. I didn't regret the choice to leave. I regretted it was *Juliet* who'd temporarily taken over my role.

She saw our cheer team as her ticket to a future with a professional athlete. An attitude I heartily disapproved of since I knew how hard the rest of my squad worked to be the best. I frowned as I brushed my teeth with my finger and Gavin's toothpaste.

Juliet wouldn't melt back into obscurity without a little help. Today's practice, the first since I returned to Addison, would give me a better idea of how much trouble I could expect from her.

After checking on Henry, who was living her best life sleeping on Cole's bed, I changed into my one set of clean workout clothes and hightailed it to Wildcat Coffee. Gavin had said something about being at practice this morning, so I didn't have to avoid my fav coffee shop.

I parked in front like I usually did and calculated my chances of making it through the line before Stephen called. Not good. People were backed up two deep at the counter, and a quick scan told me all the tables were taken. Didn't they have anywhere else to get coffee?

With a last longing look at the door, I skirted the building. Despite Gavin's intrusion into my personal breakdown —and the subsequent ill-advised kiss—I still loved the little courtyard with the broken fountain. I was just more careful now to be sure I was alone.

My regular Tuesday morning gabfest with Stephen usually took place while cuddled up in bed, but today wasn't a PJs and gossip day. Today was a boss bitch day.

I settled into my spot on the side of the fountain, tilting my face up to the sun. Warmth soaked into my cheeks, and my stiff shoulders relaxed. Gavin. Juliet. Mac. My parents. I could deal with all of them if given enough time and caffeine. All I needed was a chance to get my thoughts in order when I wasn't surrounded by Gavin's scent.

A light breeze blew my ponytail into my face, and I caught a whiff of it again. My eyes popped open as my brain finally picked out why he smelled so familiar. Rain. He smelled like rain and trees. When I was a teenager, my parents had carted us out to a posh little cabin in Oregon, one of the few times they'd tried to do something as a family.

We weren't roughing it by any means—the place had concierge services—but Mom had complained the whole time about the rainy weather and Dad had ignored us both in favor of his phone. I'd loved it. Water dripped from the trees right outside our porch, and no one followed me into the woods to demand I live up to their idea of the perfect daughter.

That feeling—the peace and serenity—that's what had crept into my chest last night and wouldn't let go. I really needed Gavin to not be the one causing it. He couldn't be trusted.

The blaring ringtone of my phone interrupted my brooding. Stephen had impeccable timing. He didn't know how out of sync my life had veered since our last talk, and I had no intention of informing him.

This time of year was always hard enough, and I didn't need him trying to take care of me. Even if I could probably use the help.

I took a deep breath and centered myself before answering the video call. "You're two minutes late."

Stephen tsked at me, a wide grin taking over his handsome face. "Good morning to you too, beautiful. I take it we skipped coffee in favor of basking today? I can get behind that."

The camera spun and Stephen plopped down into one of the cushy patio chairs on his balcony. Behind him, the skyline of downtown Austin glimmered in the sun. Unlike me, he'd stayed in town to attend the University of Texas, and his parents had gifted him a condo in the new high rise they'd built next to the lake.

The penthouse, of course. I tried not to be jealous—I'd spent the summer in my family's beach house, after all—but living as a transient for the last few weeks made me stare longingly at his patio furniture.

Stephen's face relaxed even as his blue eyes sharpened. "There. Now we're both lazing about. Why are you outside? Have you finally given in and decided to just live under the bridge in a series of interconnected boxes like a feral cat?"

I laughed, letting the stress from everything melt as much as possible in the face of Stephen's ridiculous image of my life. "Not quite. I found a place to live. It's not ideal, but it's better than Lizzy's floor."

He leaned back, swiveling slightly. "And this new place accommodates my duck bestie?"

"Yes. Henry has her own bathroom and several full-grown men coddling her."

His eyes narrowed. "Why are there several full-grown men in your new place? You didn't become a madame, did you? I mean, good for you, but... wait, is this a reverse harem situation? Are you the marshmallow in the fluffernutter sandwich?" His brows flew up. "You think any of them are interested in crossing swords? It wouldn't be the first time I've seen you naked, and I know your type. Totally worth it."

I squeezed the bridge of my nose and shook my head. A large cup of coffee would make such a huge difference in this conversation. On the best of days, I had trouble following Stephen's wild topic changes, but I was usually at least mediocre in controlling the chaos. Today, I could barely keep up.

"I'm not engaging in orgies, though I appreciate your willingness to sacrifice at the altar of my nakedness. To answer your first question, I have four male roommates, none of whom drink cold brew, so I'm outside Wildcat talking to you instead of getting my fix."

Stephen scoffed. "Girl, go inside and handle it. I'm not ready to deal with your uncaffeinated ass."

I sent a speculative look at the side of the coffee shop, then sighed. "I'll grab something on the way to practice. You'll just have to live with less fun Eva today."

"Challenge accepted. So who are you shacking up with?"

"Coffee guy."

He pursed his lips and gave me a chiding look. "You still don't know his name?"

"Why would I want to know his name? He's an asshole who refuses to follow the rules of society. Just because he has a dicktastic attitude doesn't mean he has to pull me down with him."

"So you've thought about his dick?"

I choked on my own spit. "No." Yes. Hard yes.

Stephen's voice softened. "What's his name?"

"Gavin," I muttered.

"And what's the real reason you hate him?"

My eyes shot to Stephen's on my tiny phone screen, and unease crept up my spine. "You know what happened."

He leaned over, propping his cheek on his hand. "I know what you tell everyone, but you can't fool me, sweet cheeks. You only hate someone with good reason, and rudeness isn't enough."

I glanced in the direction of Wildcat Coffee and relented when I didn't see any signs of a tall, smug hockey player. The reminder would do me good. "He's the reason Kayleigh had to leave halfway through the semester."

Stephen's mouth twisted as he leaned back and stared into the distance. "Which one was Kayleigh?"

"The freshman I was mentoring two years ago. She wasn't handling the transition to college well."

"What does that have to do with your hockey hottie?"

I rolled my eyes. "He's not *my* anything. Kayleigh didn't have the healthiest coping mechanisms. She showed up to Wildcat drunk off her ass on the way to a game. They refused to serve her any coffee and sent her back to her car to drive to the stadium. Less than two blocks later she was pulled over and arrested for drunk driving. My sources say it was Gavin who handled the situation."

His brows flew up. "She could have killed someone. You're mad at him for that?"

I blew out a breath, aware of how petty it sounded on the surface. "I'm mad at him for calling the cops instead of her friends. She was wearing her cheer uniform, Stephen. He could have stalled her and had one of us come get her. Instead, he kicked her out then called the cops."

Stephen took a slow sip of his coffee, making me regret my decision to wait. "And you've held the grudge for two years?"

"Well, he made it easy by being a dick every time we came in contact."

"Why didn't you retaliate?"

I pursed my lips. "Kayleigh asked me not to. She told me later it was the best thing that could have happened to her—forcing her to get help. I still think I could have gotten her there without making her crash and burn."

He shook his head. "Eva, I love you, but you can't fix everyone."

"I can try," I muttered.

Stephen scrubbed a hand down his face in a familiar gesture of frustration. "How did you end up living with your nemesis?"

"He offered me a room at a low moment. Henry needs stability, and I need my pillowtop mattress." I wasn't going to share the details of the deal Gavin and I had made. We hadn't discussed keeping it secret, but I wasn't eager to explain how he'd one upped me in negotiations. Or how I'd started the encounter by throwing myself at him.

Stephen eyed me as if he knew I was holding something back—he probably did—but he let it go in favor of teasing me mercilessly. "Does that mean you have the potential to see him naked?"

"No. We're sharing a house not a bedroom." I added the events from last night to my list of things to never speak of again.

"Too bad," he muttered. "Well, then the potential to see him coming fresh out of the shower in maybe just a towel? Lots of chest showing. All those muscles glistening with—"

"Stephen."

"Right. I got distracted there." He squinted at me. "Are you happy with the situation?"

"It's fine. It's great. Life is great. Henry's great. Everything's great."

"Sounds great," he deadpanned. Then he waited for me to spit out the truth.

I groaned and dropped my head in my hands. "Am I insane? Is this what crazy feels like? I mean, I could just ask my parents and they would buy me a house or a yacht or something that I could live in. Would it really be so bad to let them know I'm homeless?"

"Yes. Yes, it would. After their come to Jesus talk at the end of the summer, you made that stupid dating agreement with your dad to get him to back off. He was only worried about your lack of appropriate prospects for a future Mr. Evangeline Adams. What do you think Daddy is going to demand if he knew you were flirting with the hobo life? Play the game, girl. Sidenote: definitely don't mention the four very male roommates."

I'd managed to avoid thinking about the dating agreement while I focused on the housing problem, but Dad wouldn't wait much longer before calling it in. Now that he'd decided he wanted to be a senator, he needed his family to fall in line with the right optics, which meant his wild cheerleading daughter needed to be paired off with a stable partner who could control her.

Good luck to him. No one controlled me except me.

I ignored Stephen's advice because of course I wasn't going to tell my parents I was living with half a hockey team. "I have a prospect for the future Mr. Evangeline Adams. I have you."

"You don't have me."

"Yes, I do. You promised me in the eleventh grade you would marry me if we both hit thirty and hadn't married anyone else. Or if my parents forced me into something."

He finished his coffee and set the mug out of sight behind him. "Your parents can't force you into anything unless you let them. Dating young, rich, *acceptable* men—and your parents and I disagree heavily on the definition of that term—shouldn't be too much of a hardship for you. Get the suitors out of the way and enjoy your time with the hockey hotties, even the one you claim to hate. Nothing is too hard if you're willing to accept help from other people."

"I know that." I chewed on my lower lip and stared out at the azaleas, nonplussed at the idea of things getting so bad I'd let someone else have a say in my life. "I'm not doing a fantastic job of taking care of myself lately. What if I graduate and find out I'm not a badass outside of TU?"

Stephen sighed. "Look at me."

I shifted my unhappy gaze to his, and he shook his head. "No, not like that. You look sad and depressed. Pretend you're giving someone a pep-talk, like when you do that jersey thing with all your athlete friends."

I huffed out a breath and straightened my shoulders, resigned to Stephen's help.

He gave a sharp nod. "Better. You are going to crush the shit out of your assistantship and your dating life and your new housing situation. You're going to graduate with honors, and you're going to go out into the business world and make everyone your bitch."

I raised a brow. "You have no idea what my goals actually are, do you?"

"Is that a problem? I don't need to know about your secret spy ring to see your influence on that campus. The same tactics work everywhere."

"I don't have a secret spy ring," I said quietly.

He snorted. "Yes you do, Eva. Don't pull that demure bullshit with me. I may not know the details, but what I do know is that you succeed at everything you put your mind to, and you're going to succeed at this too. Even if you have to deal with grumpy coffee guy all year long. Think of it as practice dealing with hot assholes in the business world. Won't that be fun?"

I scrunched my nose, but he had a point. My influence at TU wasn't going to magically transfer to the real world right away, but I had every intention of cultivating a powerful reputation—with time. Before that, though, I needed to get through the challenges of the next few months.

In respect to Kayleigh's wishes, I'd kept my distance from Gavin over the last two years, going as far as to avoid Wildcat Coffee if I saw him through the window. His presence wouldn't be a problem today since he'd be at the arena, but maybe it was time I asserted my dominance over my favorite coffee shop. I couldn't let him keep getting away with the shit he pulled last night.

A grin spread over Stephen's face. "There she is. Do good in the world…"

I matched his smile and finished the motto we'd shared since the day we met. "And don't take shit from anyone."

He stood up and stretched. "Excellent. I have to go pretend to work on a group project. Keep me updated on Operation Naked Hockey Ass."

I laughed, trying desperately not to think about Gavin's chest under my fingers last night. "Needs a better name. Talk later. Love you."

"Love you too, sweet cheeks."

I tucked my phone away, in a considerably better mood than when I'd walked into the courtyard. Across from me, pink and yellow azaleas swayed softly in the breeze. Stephen always had that effect on me.

My watch beeped with my fifteen-minute warning. After the unconventional pep talk, I had just enough time to grab a coffee before I needed to head to the gym. My ponytail brushed my bare shoulders as I turned the corner to pop into Wildcat, stupidly pleased I wouldn't have to battle to get my fix.

A trio of people sitting at one of the high-top tables waved at me as I walked in. I didn't recognize them, but I waved back with a warm smile. Unlike Gavin, my default was kindness. I glanced at the counter, and my good mood faded. Momentum took me two more steps into the building before I skidded to a halt.

Standing behind the counter with a pair of fuzzy black cat ears perched on his head, Gavin smirked at me.

7

Gavin

I dropped my helmet on the bench in front of my locker just in time to catch the glove flying toward my face. My gaze shot across the room to Jake Sellers, the center for our second line and our resident gossip, and he wiggled his fingers for me to throw his glove back to him.

"Oh, you want this?" I feigned surprise, then tossed the glove over my shoulder into my locker.

Sellers snickered. "I knew you were cranky. What's with all the aggression today? This was supposed to be a *light* practice."

"I'm prepping for our first match with Easton. As you all should be. Without Thompson, our second line is weak."

Jaden Staniszweski, Thompson's former linemate, piped up from across the room. "Hey, not our fault he transferred to the frozen tundra. Killsy and I are bringing the new guy up to speed." He bumped shoulders with his other linemate, Killian Carter.

For his part, Killian gave me a distracted nod. Coach had paired them with another junior transfer from South

Dakota, though I was pretty sure he was originally from Canada, Silas Levac.

I shook my head. "Not fast enough. Tobias Kane is going to skate right past you. Don't make Mase carry your ass on the ice."

Jaden muttered something, but I didn't bother asking him to repeat himself. Instead, I focused on stripping down so I could shower and get the hell out of the locker room. Cole glanced around from his locker next to me, then lowered his voice.

"Did Danny come by after we left?"

The innocent question made my shoulders tighten to the point of pain. "Yes."

They usually dropped the subject if I didn't volunteer information, but from my other side, Reece joined in. "What did our new roommate think of your doppelganger?"

The image of Danny staring thoughtfully up the stairs in Eva's direction made my jaw lock shut. I didn't trust my brother not to fuck with me simply because he was bored, which meant he would definitely fuck with Eva if given the chance. Cole, Reece, and Mase knew the score. At least, they knew enough of it to understand I'd take care of him whether he deserved it or not.

Eva's opinion didn't matter.

"She didn't meet him."

Cole frowned. "Why not?"

I sighed, tired of having to explain myself again. "She was still asleep upstairs." I knew my mistake immediately.

Reece's grin sharpened, and he tapped his chin with his finger. "Wait, you offered her your bed last night, but you never came back down. After your little speech warning us about getting involved with Eva, I'd have expected you to last more than an hour."

I glared at him, hoping my horrible mood would be enough to convince him I wasn't involved with Eva. Anything I said would probably be a lie, and I tried not to lie to my friends. Unfortunately, Sellers had heard Reece too.

Sellers snickered. "Have you seen Eva? He's lucky he didn't come in his pants on the way up the stairs."

I threw his glove back at him. His reflexes weren't as fast as mine—something we'd have to work on—and it smacked him in the nose with a satisfying thud. "Shut it."

He spread his hands, backing out of projectile range. "I'm just saying. Let me know when you're done with her."

His attitude, one probably shared by most of my team, pushed me out of my head. I stood and whistled to get everyone's attention.

"Since Reece apparently can't keep his mouth shut for five minutes," I paused to scowl at him, but he inclined his head like I'd just complimented him. "Eva Adams moved into our extra room. I don't need any of you fucking with my roommate. Got it?"

Several heads nodded, but then Killsy raised his hand. "Can I still fuck with Cole, or is that a new house rule?"

The room exploded in laughter as Cole flipped him off. Mase made his way through the hyenas and shook his head. "You should have known better."

"I had to try to warn them off at least."

He sent me a disgusted look. "Not them. Moving her into the house. She's going to cause problems."

I pinched the bridge of my nose. "Not now, Mase. I need to shower so I can get to my class. You can tell me all about how much trouble Eva's going to be over dinner."

He shrugged and shouldered his bag, already dressed in ripped jeans and a black shirt so faded I couldn't tell what the design was supposed to be. Mase didn't shower at school. Half the time he went home before his classes started, but he'd been known to throw on some deodorant and call it good. The man did not give a single fuck.

Cole bumped my shoulder. "Are you going to invite her for the exhibition game?"

My brows drew together. "Eva?"

"Yeah. Our new roommate? It's the Friends and Family thing. I've never been able to get her to come before, but maybe she'd be willing now that she's basically family."

"She's not family." The headache that had started with Danny blossomed into a full-blown pounding at my temples. I rubbed my neck, trying to relieve the pressure.

He tilted his head at me. "Then why warn everyone off?"

"I don't want her messing with our season. We're finally playing at a top-tier level, and I want to win a championship before I leave. Eva might as well have 'drama' tattooed on her ass."

Cole raised a brow. "And it has nothing to do with the fact you *didn't* come back down last night? You know you could have crashed in one of our rooms if you needed to."

He was savvy enough to realize Eva sleeping in one of their rooms was a horrible idea, but I didn't have a good reason to give him for my choice. I'd been planning to torture her a little before grabbing the floor anywhere else. Then she'd had to open her mouth.

I didn't know why I let her get under my skin. Eva was a problem, and avoiding her was the only viable solution at this point. Something I needed to remember if I didn't want to fuck everything up.

Instead of answering Cole, I gave him a tight smile and headed for the showers.

I MADE it to my class on time. Barely. Too bad I couldn't pay attention for shit. I was going the easy route and getting a degree in general studies. Yes, I knew it was a bullshit major, but it gave me the flexibility I needed to dedicate my time to cleaning up after Danny in addition to playing hockey.

To be honest, I hadn't planned to graduate. I'd intended to play a couple of years then get called up to Dallas. That was before everything went to hell my senior year of high school. I wasn't even supposed to be at TU. I'd gotten into the University of Ohio, where I'd been living while playing Juniors hockey, but when they revoked my scholarship, I didn't have a lot of options.

Luckily, TU was looking to build a winning team by recruiting the fuckups and the rebels. Coach jokingly called us the bad boys of hockey. I just wanted to forget the mess and play. The exhibition game was in two weeks, and our first real game was only a few weeks after that. We had a lot of work to do before then.

Morning practice meant my afternoon was mostly free. I needed to hit the weight room three times this week, but I wasn't feeling it. My car was parked by the rink, meaning I needed to walk across campus. I'd count the hike as my bonus cardio for the day.

September in Texas was hot as balls, so by the time I got to my car, I felt like I needed a third shower. The fantasy from this morning of Eva spread on the bathroom counter flitted into my mind like it belonged there, and I swore. No more showers today.

Hot air billowed past me when I opened the door. I shook my head and reached inside to crank the AC. My car was a sauna, Danny was skipping classes again, and I wanted to fuck my newest roommate. Not a phrase I ever thought I'd utter, even in my mind. I'd been one hundred percent serious when I told her my dick wasn't part of the deal, despite all the back and forth.

Hockey season meant not splitting my focus by getting involved with women. The occasional hook up to relieve pressure, sure, but never anyone I knew. Too much risk of a distraction. Eva was already going to be hell on my system, I absolutely couldn't add sex into the mix.

My phone buzzed as I finished making excuses to my dick. I checked the screen and groaned at the name. Carter was an agent and a family friend, in that order. Even after the scandal, he stood by me. I hadn't officially signed with him because of college sports restrictions, but he offered regular guidance, whether I wanted it or not.

> Carter: Just talked to Dallas.

Me: Anything new?

> Carter: They want to see TU in the playoffs this year.

Me: We will be.

> Carter: Even better if you win. They're still hedging.

Me: It was 3 yrs ago. I've been staying under the radar since.

> Carter: That's the problem. You're laying too low.

Me: I'm doing what you told me.

> Carter: Now I'm telling you something different. Dallas wants to see what you can do with an underdog team. So stop holding back.

I gritted my teeth and shoved my phone in my pocket before I followed his advice by telling him to go fuck himself. Dallas almost dropped me because I was too much of a risk, and now they wanted me to stop playing it safe?

Sometimes I wondered if all the bullshit was worth the payoff.

Mom's voice popped into my head like it always did when I started feeling doubts. *Do what you love, baby, and don't let anyone take it away from you. Not even yourself.* She'd told me that when I'd been nervous about living with strangers in another state to play Juniors hockey. I sometimes wondered if she'd give me the same advice knowing what it would cost me—and them.

Fuck, all the stress was getting to me. I needed to get some sleep, alone, and get my head on straight, just like I'd told the team this morning. With any luck, Eva would be gone from the house doing whatever she did during the day, and I could take a nap before starting the homework I hadn't paid attention to in class.

Ten minutes later, I cursed as I had to street park in front of my house. A moving truck was taking up the driveway, and three big guys in coveralls were talking to Cole. I slammed out of my car, already prepared for battle, but Cole took one look at my face and headed me off before I could get past the sidewalk.

"Where's Eva?" I demanded.

Cole held up both hands. "Not here. She asked me to handle the movers."

At least one thing was going right today. "How much longer are they going to be?"

"They're almost done, the fridge is stocked with basics and premade meals, and the duck is sleeping in my room with the door closed. I'm handling it. Go get some food before you tear off someone's head."

I grumbled at the lack of anything to be pissed about and sidestepped Cole. "I'm grabbing a nap. I'll eat after."

"She's not the enemy, you know," he called after me.

I didn't bother turning around. "Don't care."

Cole's laugh followed me into the house.

8

Eva

Operation Naked Hockey Ass was officially on hiatus. I'm not ashamed to admit I turned on my heel the second I saw Gavin and fled Wildcat Coffee. Then I avoided him for a full week. How? Through extensive and flagrant exploitation of my friendship with Cole.

Gavin, for his part, didn't seem too eager to search me out. I made sure the boys had food and the house was clean, as per our deal, so he had no reason to talk to me. Certainly, he had no reason to lie to me again about his practice time.

And yet, the only words he'd said to me all week were to inform me I needed to move my car so they could go to practice this morning. Standing outside Wildcat Coffee, staring in the window at Gavin's profile as he flirted with the redhead next to him, I shook my head. Why?

What was the point of convincing me he was going to practice then coming to work here?

Instead of marching in there and demanding answers, I got back in my car and drove to the athletic center. There was a vending machine with woefully subpar cappuccino on the administration floor, and I had cheer practice in twenty minutes.

I knew, underneath the righteous annoyance, that I was using his little white lies to create distance after the night I spent with him. Gavin had proven more than once he wasn't trustworthy, despite the stupid little flutters in my stomach every time I got a glimpse of him walking around the house without a shirt.

With a last disgusting glug, the vending machine spit my lukewarm coffee into a paper cup. It didn't smell too bad, but the acrid taste wasn't entirely masked by the massive amount of added sugar. I tried not to breathe through my nose while I chugged it on my way to the practice field. At this point, I'd take a caffeine hit straight to a vein.

Once my bed and other furniture was delivered, I'd been sleeping fine... except for the random middle of the night glimpses when I wanted water or needed to use the bathroom—the shared bathroom Gavin hadn't warned me about.

At least he usually kept the door on his side closed, but twice he'd forgotten and I had to dig Henry out of a pile of clothes on Gavin's bedroom floor while he slept. The silly duck thought she was nesting, but I couldn't blame her. That first morning, I'd wrapped myself in blankets that smelled like him and curled up in the middle of his bed.

Hence the need for distance and perspective. I'd clearly lost mine.

The squad was already on the field stretching by the time I rolled up, and there was Juliet, front and center like she owned the place. Her long brunette hair sported a soft curl as it cascaded down the back of her sundress, and I badly wanted to roll my eyes. She couldn't practice her own stunting in a dress. Twice now I'd had to remind her we were leaders by example, meaning we had to do the work too. Looked like I'd be upping the count to three.

Several gazes looked past her as I dropped my bag at the edge of the grass and chucked the last of the sad coffee in the trash can. Juliet turned with her hands on her hips, and I sent her a wide, friendly smile even though I wanted to point out her full face of makeup was wasted since the football players were at the stadium working on endurance.

She gave me a wan smile in return. "Glad you could make it today, Eva. We've already started, but there's room in the back."

I laughed and plopped down next to her in front of the group. "I'm fine here. Thanks."

Behind the cheerleaders, Coach Kat pursed her lips to hide a smile. After my illustrious return, Kat had set me and Juliet up as co-captains this year. I didn't mind sharing the leadership duties, but Juliet tested my last nerve at every practice.

She lowered herself to the grass next to me, and we managed to get through warmups with no verbal bloodshed. Our squad met three times a week for stunt practice and twice more for weight training and endurance. Since cheerleading wasn't considered a sport at the college level, no one cared how often we practiced—and we practiced our asses off.

We were a co-ed group that competed at the highest level, and we'd won Nationals all three years I'd been at TU. I planned to make it a perfect four out of four. If Juliet would get out of my way and let me choreograph a mind-blowing fucking routine.

On cue, Juliet pulled me aside to start picking apart the decisions we'd made last week about the stunt list. "Eva, I need to talk to you about the transition between the second and third stunts."

We performed some of the most difficult stunting legally allowed in competitive cheerleading, but Juliet would prefer stunts that were easier to perfect. I held up a hand, stopping her before she could launch into her reasons why my transitions weren't good enough.

"I'm happy to discuss the choreo, but not right now. I need to practice my stunts like everyone else. Text me after practice and we'll find a time to talk."

I didn't give her a chance to argue before I walked away to join the bases in my first configuration. Juliet left me alone to work on her own stunts, but I could hear her lecturing the other members of her group. Unfortunately, she wasn't wrong. Juliet was a talented cheerleader, and she knew her stuff. If only she dedicated that knowledge to making our whole squad better instead of using her co-captain position to boost her standing with the football players.

Practice ended as it always did, with Kat going over a list of pointers to work on for next time. Juliet practically preened when Kat mentioned the transitions, but no one else seemed to notice. I had a few things to add to her list, but I didn't have time to stay and talk since I had an appointment to get to in the Anderson Business College, or the ABC as we all called it.

I was meeting with Carl Bennington, my consumer behavior professor. Professor Bennington was only a few years older than me, but he'd been fast tracked through business school and given a position here based on his firm's impressive achievements—and probably their hefty support of the business school.

He only taught one class a semester, an upper-level business lecture, and once a year he took on an assistant to help him with a project at his firm. I'd applied over the summer, blatantly using my dad's name to get my foot in the door. Since the final student was chosen by a committee, I didn't consider it cheating when I won the assistantship.

Normally, I'd have introduced myself after our first class last week, but I'd been wearing clothes from the day before thanks to the moving snafu. Not a big deal considering we weren't supposed to officially start until October. Instead, I'd emailed about the assistantship. After several days, he'd given me a date and time to show up at his office on campus. The whole exchange felt a little like a lord speaking to a peon, but I'd been reading a lot of historical romance lately.

His office was large and bright, probably more than he needed to teach one class a semester, but I wasn't going to argue the politics of office assignments in a posh college. It was also meticulously organized with only a single small picture frame on display. Carl Bennington matched his office perfectly. Bland and forgettable despite the well-tailored suit he wore.

I knocked on the open door, and his eyes flicked toward me.

"Come in."

"Professor Bennington, it's nice to officially meet you." I held out my hand, but after a brief glance at my shorts and tank top, he returned his attention to the tablet in front of him. Not a great beginning. I dropped my arm and waited for him to finish whatever he was doing.

Except he didn't. He nodded at the chairs in front of his desk without looking up again.

"Ms. Adams, I understand you're eager to begin the assistantship, so have a seat."

"Thank you." I didn't like the vibe I was getting, but

polite was my default to business associates. "I'd like to discuss my responsibilities this semester so I can plan the rest of my time accordingly."

He hummed absently. "You'll have five to ten hours a week of work assigned by me through email. You'll also accompany me to several meetings with clients over the course of the semester, to be determined at a later date. We'll, of course, work around your school schedule, but you may have to miss extracurriculars if you're needed elsewhere."

I fought to keep the frown off my face. "I'll try my best to attend any necessary meetings."

His mouth tightened a smidge, though he still didn't address me directly. "You must be excited to get some real-world experience before leaving college. I'd advise you to make this assistantship a priority."

The offhand remark told me he either hadn't read my carefully prepared application, or he didn't care. Through sheer force of will, I kept my tone upbeat.

"Oh, I have experience. I worked with the Delacourt Cheer Center over the summer developing a new social media outreach program and reorganizing their business plan to better fit their goals." I'd also taught cheer classes, but I didn't get the feeling he was interested in the hands-on aspect I enjoyed at that job.

Even without me adding in the physical work, he waved his hand dismissively. "I'm sure the cheer company was fun, but my firm works with real businesses. Right now, we're contracted for a major marketing push with Zodiac Diamonds."

I was probably supposed to be impressed by him name dropping one of the most well-known jewelry companies in the world, but money never impressed me. I had plenty of it already. Just like I recognized a power play when I saw it. Keeping his attention on his tablet was his way of showing me how unimportant I was compared to his time.

Disappointment and his shitty attitude stole any excitement I'd had from winning the assistantship, but I knew how to deal with his type. He expected me to do the majority of the work in the conversation, then I'd be grateful when he deigned to respond and not ask any questions.

I knew this game because I'd played it plenty of times—and I didn't lose.

If he insisted on ignoring me, I'd sit here in his uncomfortable chair and run through our stunt routine in my head. I kept my eyes on him, with a polite smile on my face, and tried to create the most outlandish, dangerous stunt I could think of. Bonus points if it made the vein in Juliet's temple throb when I suggested it.

As usual, turning the silent treatment back on someone worked wonderfully. Most people who employed it weren't able to effectively deal with it being reversed on them. My good buddy Carl was no exception.

He finally set his tablet on the desk in front of him and studied me. In the back of my mind, a warning bell went off.

"I understand your father is undertaking a run for Congress."

In a flash, several key points connected in my mind. This summer, my dad, a shrewd and wildly successful businessman, had announced quietly to his family and friends he was going into politics. Shortly after, I'd been chosen as a finalist for the assistantship.

Dammit. I'd really wanted this to be a positive experience.

"That's something you'll have to discuss with him. Is

there anything you need from me in the next few weeks for the assistantship?"

Carl's eyes sharpened and he nodded. "I understand, and no. The project I have in mind for you is still slated for an October start date."

I was highly skeptical any project he picked for me would be worth my time, but I didn't like doing things in half measures. If my name was going to be associated with this, I would kick ass at it. As soon as I knew what it was.

"Could I have access to the background information for the project so I can get myself up to speed before the real work begins?"

He laughed. "That won't be necessary. I'm sure you have plenty of formal cocktail attire in your closet."

My smile felt brittle, but I refused to react to his insinuation my role would be to play dress up. I knew two of the previous assistantship winners, and they'd had challenging months-long projects to work on. Then again, they were both male.

I hadn't been prepared for the misogyny, but I should have been. Unfortunately, Carl, who no longer deserved any title of respect, still had control over my grade for the semester and any recommendations that came from this project, no matter how insulting the work may turn out to be.

"Thank you for your time. Please let me know when you expect to have a project ready for me." I stood to leave, and he picked up his tablet again. Before he lifted it out of my view, I saw he'd been scrolling the school's social media.

Fuck this guy. Too bad for him I wasn't the learn-from-the-experience-and-move-on type—I was the wait-for-the-right-moment-and-take-revenge type. As long as he was in control of my grade, I'd play his game. But in a few months,

I'd be free, and he'd have given me access to a major project at his firm.

Carl Bennington would be useless to me. I had no intention of taking a job with him, but I'd take great pleasure in using him as a stepping stone to a better company.

9

Gavin

I was hiding from a girl. Not just any girl—we've all had that moment with an aggressive puck bunny—but the annoyingly beautiful girl I shared a bathroom with. Reece would lose his shit if he knew. In his mind, you run toward women, not away.

My bedroom door was cracked so I could hear the raspy sound of Eva's voice at the bottom of the stairs, but I couldn't make out the actual words. After the fiasco at practice, I'd gone out of my way to avoid any contact with her.

I'd expected her to take advantage of my absence by shirking her duties, but the fridge and pantry were stocked and the house was clean. She didn't whine or complain, and even Mase seemed to have gotten used to her. As a bonus, we traded in Reece's questionable cooking skills for really good premade meals. Honestly, we should have moved a rich girl in years ago.

The bathroom was becoming a problem though. Over the last week and a half, I could hear the water running every time she turned on the shower, and when she left her bathroom door open, I could see directly into her room.

Cleaner than I thought it'd be but just as girly. She went for a lot of white and light green with pink things scattered around. Her furniture was light colored wood and expensive looking. To be fair, everything in there was expensive looking. It even smelled expensive. A light scent that reminded me of fresh air without being overpowering. Personally, I preferred the cinnamon and vanilla smell she'd left all over my bed.

Stupidly, I hadn't washed my sheets yet. I should—I *definitely* should—but I hadn't gotten around to it. To my surprise, Eva hadn't caused any drama in the house.

The duck had made herself at home in my room from time to time when her owner wasn't around. Honestly, Henry was cute, and I didn't mind the company as long as she wore the weird little diapers Eva kept putting on her.

Today, though, Henry was downstairs somewhere, and Eva was laughing at whichever of my asshole roommates was pushing the boundaries of our friendship. I'd told them. She's here as a last resort. Don't adopt her.

She laughed again, and the sound of the door slamming shut cut it off. A strained silence followed, then I heard Danny's voice. Fuck. I took off down the stairs, completely abandoning my plan to avoid Eva until she moved out or graduated.

I skidded to a stop in the living room and took a second to get my bearings. Of course, it was all of them. Even Mase was getting in on the action. He had his back to the room while he ate, but I knew him. If he wasn't interested, he'd have taken his food downstairs. Eva was sitting on the couch, sandwiched between Cole and Reece, though neither of them was touching her, and all three were staring at Danny, who had a shit eating grin on his face.

The asshole was wearing my favorite shirt again. TU

hockey was emblazoned on the front, and he was all sweaty, as if he'd just come from practice. Since I hadn't heard his motorcycle, my bet was he'd walked here from Wildcat and wanted a ride somewhere. As I watched Danny's gaze lift from Eva to me, Henry waddled over from the kitchen and quacked at my feet.

Eva's head whipped around, and her mouth formed an O.

Danny chuckled. "I guess you didn't tell her about me. That explains all the scowling when she comes in to get coffee."

Eva's icy eyes speared in my direction, but I didn't offer an explanation. Disappointment flashed there for a split second before she turned back to my brother. "Who are you?"

Cole spared me a glance, and I nodded for him to go ahead and tell her. "Danny King, Gavin's brother. He goes to TU too, and I'm guessing you already know he works at Wildcat Coffee."

Eva glared at everyone in the living room, even the back of Mase's head, as Danny leaned against the wall, soaking in the drama he'd caused. "No one thought to tell me?"

Reece wisely stayed silent, but Cole took the hit. "It's not a big deal."

She sent him a wounded look. "It's not a big deal you lied to me?"

He winced. "Sorry, Eva, but I thought you knew."

"You thought I knew Gavin was an evil twin?"

"You know everything. How could you have missed that?"

She grunted in frustration. "Because I purposely avoid learning anything about my asshole nemesis."

Henry sat on my foot, demanding attention, so I scooped her up before joining the rest of them in the living room. "Can't stop thinking about me, huh?"

She stared at the ceiling for a five count, probably imagining her hands around my neck. I wouldn't mind a little throat play, but it wouldn't be her hands around *my* throat. I pushed the image out of my mind and dumped her duck in her lap.

Danny didn't miss the exchange, and his brows went up. "So it *is* like that. I thought so."

Both Eva and I glared at him, but neither of us denied it. Why would we? It should be obvious to anyone with eyeballs we hated each other.

"What do you need?" I asked him instead.

"A ride. Motorcycle's in the shop, and I have a shift tonight at Greenfield."

I reared back. "I didn't know you were working at Greenfield."

The ice rink was on the poorer side of town near the bars and Papi's Taco Stand. It must have been built more than twenty years ago, but the Greenfield family kept it running for the locals. I'd been there a couple of times when TU was doing maintenance work on our rink.

He shrugged. "Guess you don't know everything either."

Mase stood from his spot. "I'll take you. I need to run some errands anyway." He put his bowl in the sink and nodded at the door. "You ready now?"

Danny cut his eyes to Eva, but he must have thought better of whatever crossed his mind. "Sure," he told Mase.

"Thanks," I mumbled, and Mase slapped my shoulder as he walked past.

The door closed to silence again, but this time I was

downstairs in the middle of it. Exactly where I'd promised myself not to be. I crossed my arms and narrowed my eyes at my two best friends sitting on either side of the woman who hated my guts.

"What's going on?"

Reece gave me wide, innocent eyes. "Nothing. Absolutely nothing. Cole and I were going to play some NHL14, but Eva was watching a trick competition—"

"Stunt," she interrupted.

"Stunt competition," Reece continued as if she hadn't said anything. "And these guys are doing crazy shit. We kind of got hooked. You should check it out."

He draped his arm along the back of the couch behind Eva, and I shifted my gaze to Cole who was nodding along.

"I thought we had an agreement."

Cole laughed. "No, you issued an ultimatum, and we didn't say anything. I was friends with her before you moved her in here. I'm not going to stop just because she has your panties in a twist."

Eva's lips tipped up in a smug little smile. "I love a man who thinks for himself."

Henry made a chittering noise that sounded like agreement. Traitor. I thought we'd come to an understanding when I let her invade my shower on Wednesday, but she was staring adoringly at Cole from Eva's lap.

Reece slid closer, toying with the pink strands in her hair. "I'm always thinking for myself. Like right now, I'm thinking if you're free tonight—"

"No." I growled.

He shrugged. "No harm in trying."

"Move. Now." I barely gave Reece time to vacate before I claimed the spot next to Eva. Several inches closer than Reece had been sitting.

She looked at me expectantly.

"What?" I grumbled.

"Ah, there it is. I was wondering when you'd turn your one-word charm on me."

Eva had been laughing and having fun with the others, but with me, the words caught fire. We couldn't be near each other for more than a few minutes without clashing, and I was tired of the constant battle. Of course, that didn't stop me from firing back.

I leaned down, close enough our noses almost touched. "I thought you weren't interested in my charms, Princess?"

Her eyes narrowed, and the heat in them nearly scorched me. "You're the one who interrupted us, and you're free to leave any time."

"This is my living room."

"I live here too, and I was here first." She made a shooing motion with her hand, and I grinned.

Nothing would make me move from this couch before she did. "I'm sure you can learn to share. I'm suddenly interested in learning about stunting."

A tiny growl came out of her throat, and I desperately wanted to hear the noise again in other circumstances. "Why don't you go take another shower? Maybe relieve some pressure and come back less of a jackass."

I'd wondered if she could hear me, and now I had my answer. The thought of Eva listening as I jacked off took me from half-mast to hard as a rock, and I'd bet my good gloves her uneven breathing wasn't from anger. She was as turned on as I was. Maybe next time I'd say her name out loud.

"You're going to need to try harder if you want to scare me away."

Her chin jutted out, tilting her face up to mine. "I'm not trying anything. I'm simply pointing out your rudeness."

I tucked my hand under her fall of hair, stroking my thumb across the back of her neck. "I have a better use for your mouth."

Her eyes dilated, and the air between us crackled with electricity. She didn't move away, not a single inch. From her lap, Henry gave a disgruntled quack, and I suddenly remembered we weren't alone in the room. Given another second, I'd have said to hell with the consequences and taken what she was offering. Why the fuck couldn't I keep my hands off her?

The couch jostled as Reece stood from his spot. "A shower sounds good. Let me know the next time you need to study film. I have a big screen in my room we could use."

My fingers tightened on her neck. "The hell you will," I muttered.

Neither of us looked his way as he clomped up the stairs, but Cole got up to yank Henry away from Eva. I slid my gaze toward him without letting her go. He nailed us both with a sharp glare.

"Okay, time out. I'd rather wax my balls than be here while you two engage in whatever the hell foreplay this is. Can you behave while I'm in the room or do I need to chase after Reece?"

Eva's brow quirked a tiny bit, questioning whether or not I could control myself, and I released her to lean back. I couldn't even deny it was foreplay after the stupid shit I'd said. "I'll behave if she will."

Cole waited for Eva to nod before saying, "Excellent, because now's a good time."

My brows drew together as I tried to wrench my mind out of the gutter. "What?"

"The exhibition game? Friends and family? Any of this

ringing a bell?" He rolled his eyes. "Nevermind, I'll handle it."

Eva's gaze bounced between us before she echoed me. "What?"

Cole grinned. "Before the season starts, we do an exhibition game against a local team. We usually kick their asses, but it's a nice introduction to the sport. They give us tickets to hand out, and they do this whole hot cocoa thing before the game. Weird if you ask me, since it's not exactly cold here, but it can get chilly in the arena."

Eva blinked slowly. "You want me to come to a hockey game?"

"Yeah. It's on a Friday so you won't be cheering, and it'll be fun. You can have my ticket, and I have an extra jersey you could wear."

Her eyes flicked toward me for the briefest second, then she smiled at him. "Sure. I'd love to support you guys, but I draw the line at wearing a hockey jersey. I have a reputation to protect after all."

Cole laughed, and some of the tension in my shoulders released. I kept denying any claim on Eva, but every time someone else tried to step in—anyone else, even my best friends—I clenched up. Whatever this thing was between me and her, I needed to get a grip before I took a swing at someone.

And now she was coming to our first game. Fantastic. So much for my plan to avoid her and hope my bullshit rule about not fucking them was enough to keep her away from the guys. I should have known she'd insert herself into our lives.

Cole took his seat next to Eva, and she unpaused the stunt thing she was watching. When she turned to explain something to him, her hair trailed over my wrist, and I had to adjust myself again. She'd seemingly forgotten our heated moment, but it was all I could do not to fist my hand in those pink streaks and remind her.

Eva hadn't responded to my comment about her mouth, and my dick was having a field day with the possibilities. I clearly couldn't keep ignoring her if being in a room together—not even alone—sparked this kind of reaction.

She'd surprised me by sticking to our deal and being nice to the guys despite my shitty attitude. I was willing to admit maybe she wasn't as spoiled as I'd thought, but I wasn't willing to fully trust her.

Eva had never given any indication she cared about anything other than herself until I'd found her in that courtyard. But she cared about Henry. She'd taken my deal, as humiliating as I could make it for her, to give her duck a place to live.

I may have been avoiding her, but I'd also been paying attention. She teased Reece without flirting with him, she patiently explained the stunt thing to Cole when he asked questions, and she let Mase stay in his head when he needed the time. Fuck, I was the asshole in all this, wasn't I?

I flipped my wrist to sift her silky strands through my fingers. After meeting Danny tonight, it wouldn't take her long to figure out the situation at Wildcat. The easy solution there was for me to stop covering his shifts. Up until tonight, I'd thought he didn't give a shit where his life was going, but if he'd gotten a second job, he might finally be growing up. About fucking time.

And it was about time I stopped hiding from my roommate. She glanced my way, pulling her hair from my hand, and I didn't bother pretending I wasn't watching her. Our gazes clashed, a battle for dominance underscored with fiery hunger. Something shifted between us, and she looked away first.

Yeah, Eva had a reputation for control, but I could handle her.

10

Gavin

For the first time since Eva moved in, I didn't get up early and leave before her. The morning workout was optional, and I had plenty of time before I had to be at the rink for practice. The others had already left, with Cole sending me a suspicious look on his way out.

I ignored him and sat at the table with my breakfast smoothie and my old econ textbook to study for Danny's test.

Eva's steps hesitated as she came down the stairs and saw me, but nothing stood between her and her coffee in the mornings. She breezed past me to take one of her glass bottles out of the fridge and chug half of it standing there with the door open.

With a satisfied sigh that traveled straight to my dick, she bumped the door closed with her hip. I didn't lift my eyes from the same sentence I'd been staring at since she walked into the room, but I tracked her with my peripheral vision.

Tiny, skin-tight, red shorts cupped her ass under a cropped tank top with Wildcats scrawled across her chest. I caught a hint of cut abs before she grabbed her designer backpack off the floor and waltzed to the door. Her hips swayed as if she knew I was watching, and she caught me staring at her ass a second later when she glanced over her shoulder.

I took my time meeting her gaze, not at all sorry. "I told you turnabout was fair play."

"Good morning to you too," she muttered, then shut the door behind her.

She came back in less than a minute later with her phone pressed to her ear. "Don't patronize me, David. I pay you so I don't have to know anything about cars. It won't start. I need you to fix it."

I sat back and crossed my arms over my chest, earning a quick glare from her.

Her eyes closed and she pinched the bridge of her nose. "Fine. It's parked on the street in front of the house. Call me when you know something, please."

She hung up and immediately started scrolling.

"Problem?" I asked blandly.

Eva shook her head without looking up. "My car won't start. David, my mechanic, can't get to it until tomorrow, and I have practice in twenty minutes. Why are there no Ubers around when I need them?"

I snorted. "Because we live in a college town and the drivers know the real money is at bar close. They're all sleeping."

She dropped her arm to her side with a resigned sigh. "You're not helpful, even if you're right."

"I can be helpful." I closed the book and set my empty smoothie cup in the sink. "Let's go. I'll give you a ride."

Those ice blue eyes zeroed in on me with a suspicious look insultingly similar to Cole's. "Why?"

"You told me to come back less of a jackass. I thought I'd try it since you asked so nicely. Do you want a ride or not?"

Eva shoved her phone into the side pocket of her bag and slung it over her shoulder. "Okay, I can roll with this. Practice is at the athletic center, Jeeves."

I chuckled as I followed close behind her out the door. "I knew you liked it when I called you Princess."

Her shoulders stiffened a tiny bit, but she threw a bored look at me. "You can call me whatever you want as long as you get me to practice on time. I have an upstart cheerleader to crush."

I admit, she piqued my curiosity, but I managed not to ask. Eva threw her bag in the back and buckled in before leaning against the headrest with her eyes closed. The athletic center was only a couple minutes away, on the side of campus closer to us than the rink.

As I stopped at the single traffic light between our house and campus, Eva rolled her head toward me and asked the question I'd been expecting for the last twelve hours.

"What's the story with you and your brother?"

My lips twisted as I considered my options. If I told her nothing, she'd latch on and start digging, but if I gave her something small, she might be satisfied enough to focus on her own problems. I wasn't sure what she was looking for though. The light changed, and I drove the next block and a half to the athletic center with her gaze on me.

I pulled in and stopped in one of the rare shady spots at the edge of the parking lot. Shadows from the leafy branches above us swayed in the breeze, and the surrounding forest, thick with greenery at the end of the summer, made it seem like we were alone in the world, at least for a little bit.

Neither of us made a move to get out as I shifted to face

her. "What do you want to know?"

"Which of you works at Wildcat?"

That one was easy. She could get the information in half a second by asking anyone who worked there. "He does."

"But not always."

I gave a dry laugh. "No."

"You work his shifts sometimes. That first night, that was you."

"That was me," I confirmed, but I didn't admit to the rest of it.

"Why?"

I looked past her at the trees. That was a tougher question. "He's my little brother. If he needs my help, I'm always going to say yes."

Her forehead scrunched. "I thought you were twins?"

"I'm older by two and a half minutes."

She nodded. "Yeah, that checks out. You're too bossy to be anything but a first-born child."

I sighed. "He's going to make a play for you. I need you to tell him no."

Eva laughed and tucked a long, limber leg under her. "I'm already following your stupid hands-off rule with the roomies. I don't need you taco blocking me with anyone else. You have your showers and whatever puck bunny throws herself at you. I haven't gotten off in months."

My brows shot up. "Months?"

She leaned forward with wide eyes. "Months. Indiana Bones isn't cutting it lately, and I'm not bringing a rando home to my four massive hockey player roommates who have no concept of personal space."

I made a mental note to thank Cole and Reece for being annoying. No way had Mase been involved in any personal space invasions. He didn't like being touched most days.

"I could help you with that." The offer was out of my mouth before I could stop myself.

The pulse in her neck went wild, and she tilted her head to study me. "Why?"

Because I went to bed every night with her scent invading my head, and I'd been fucking my hand for weeks pretending it was her. I couldn't tell her that though, couldn't give her that much power in our battle of wills. Instead, I deflected.

"I like being helpful."

She scoffed, but she didn't say no. "I thought your dick wasn't part of the deal."

I laughed. "I don't need my dick to get you off. How long do you have?"

Eva's eyes flicked to the windows then back to me. "Here? Anyone could see us."

I didn't give a fuck if the entire hockey team walked by as long as I could get my hands on her. "I'd better make it good then."

A slow smile curved along her lips. "You have ten minutes."

Challenge accepted. In a blink, I shifted the seat back and hauled her across the console to straddle my lap. Her hands landed on my shoulders as I fisted her hair the way I'd been imagining since last night.

Like the first kiss, heat exploded when I took her mouth. Fuck, she tasted good. I splayed my hand along the warm skin of her lower back, pulling her forward until she hit my cock, rock hard in my athletic shorts. One little upward thrust, and she whimpered, rolling her hips.

"I should never have kissed you," she muttered under her breath while rubbing herself against me.

"But you did. No going back now, Princess. You going to

let me touch you?"

She met my eyes, her breath coming in jagged little pants. "Yes, but this doesn't mean I like you. One and done, Gavin."

I leaned forward to nip at her jaw. "I'll keep that in mind for next time."

"There won't be a next time."

With her grinding on my dick, I wasn't about to take offense at her insistence. Hell, I was thinking the same thing since I'd managed to convince myself we could get this out of the way and move on.

I let her set the pace, working herself up until her head dropped back and her nails dug into my shoulders. With her back arched, her breasts were at the perfect height for my mouth, and I desperately wished I'd won more than ten minutes so I could get her naked.

I flicked a hard nipple with my tongue. "You need to come, baby?"

"God, yes," she moaned. "I'm so close…"

I dipped my head to suck at the side of her neck, eliciting another low moan. "Then it's my turn."

I tucked my hand inside the back of her tiny shorts, palming her pert ass on the way down. She shivered when I teased her tight ring of muscle, pushing back against my fingers, and I filed the info away for later. Today, though, was going to be quick and dirty. Eva needed to get off, and I was happy to oblige.

Eva ground against my cock, one hand locked behind my neck and the other fisted on my chest. Her eyes fell closed as she rocked, and when I found her soaking wet, she gasped. My finger slid in easily as I matched her rhythm.

"That's my good girl," I whispered into her ear. "You're so wet for me. Can you take another?"

She nodded roughly, and I pushed a second finger into her. Her muscles tightened around me, and I could only imagine how good this would feel on my cock. I wanted to free myself and thrust into her, use my fingers on her ass until she squeezed me everywhere.

I'd take her riding my hand and grinding against me until she came. God, I wanted to see her come. I curled my fingers a little, and she shuddered.

"Fuck, Gavin," she gasped, letting out a breathy moan.

Her head dropped to my shoulder, and her hips moved in jerky little circles as I took over. "Yeah, baby. Come all over my fucking hand. I want you so wet your squad knows exactly what you were doing before you walked in to practice."

The orgasm hit her like a lightning strike, sudden and intense. Her nails dug into my skin, and she stiffened while all her little muscles pulsed around me. I couldn't take my eyes off her. Cheeks flushed, lower lip trembling, beautiful and open.

I waited for the last aftershocks to fade before pulling my hand free of her shorts. She let out a tiny puff of air and nuzzled into my neck. This was the real Eva. Relaxed and vulnerable. The one I saw in glimpses here and there when she thought I wasn't looking.

Fuck me. One and done was never going to be enough.

I held her there, curled around me as our breathing returned to normal, knowing I could never have this version of her. Not with all the secrets between us. The moment only lasted a few seconds, then the Eva I knew returned. She leaned away from me and patted my chest with a little smile.

"Thanks. I needed that."

"Anytime," I murmured as she climbed back to her side of the car.

Eva twisted to grab her bag from the back, face still stained pink, and I made a stupid decision—I wanted more than one. She got out of the car and walked toward the facility without looking back, leaving me reeling.

I should have left it at that. I should have buried my reaction to her and driven back to the house, but I didn't. With her smell all over me, I had to get out of the car before I could calm my raging hard on. As soon as I could walk normally, I followed Eva into the athletic facility.

It didn't take much to find the gym where they were practicing. I'd waited long enough after she left that they'd already finished stretching. The group was a lot bigger than I thought it'd be, spread all over the gym and separated into three person clumps. I clung to the shadows by the door and leaned against the wall looking for Eva.

After a second, I found her, standing on one leg as a big dude held her in the air with a single arm. I wasn't the only one watching. Another girl with long dark hair braided down her back stood off to the side, scowling at Eva as she yelled something. The guy tossed her a little higher, and Eva twisted as she fell. He caught her waist, and she landed gently in front of him.

The big guy took two steps back, and Eva did some gymnastics shit into his hands. He tossed her in the air mid flip, and she spun around on his hands, coming to a stop facing the door with her arms up and a big smile on her face.

My heart pounded watching her fly through the air like that, but Eva was solid, standing on his hand like she was on the ground. The angry brunette shook her head, and Eva's mouth tightened for a split second. I sucked in a breath as the guy under her wobbled, and Eva fell sideways.

In the half a second before the two guys caught her, I

took two steps forward. I don't know what I was thinking—there was no way I could have reached her—but my chest clenched up at the thought of her hitting the ground. She laughed and patted the shoulder of the one who'd dropped her. With a sharp smile, she headed right past the brunette to grab a bottle of water from her stuff.

Why the fuck was I here? I'd offered her an orgasm, and she'd accepted. Nothing more. I wasn't one of her groupies—it shouldn't matter that ten minutes with her in the car had been the hottest encounter of my life without even getting off, and she'd thanked me as if I'd delivered a pizza. One and done. That was how she wanted it.

And Eva always got what she wanted.

Still, I'd be an asshole if I left her stranded here. I shook my head as I scooted a little farther into the shadows and found her contact on my phone.

> Me: Text me when you're done

Her gaze darted to her bag, and she squatted to pull out her phone, frowning at the message.

> Princess: Don't worry. I'll find a ride home

Before I could respond, she tossed her phone into her bag and jogged back to her partner. Fine. I had practice anyway, but she couldn't avoid me forever. We shared a bathroom. Besides, distracting her with orgasms was a much better plan than ignoring her and hoping she didn't get curious.

A smile crept over my face as I walked to my car. One and done. Except I didn't want to be done, and Eva had no idea what kind of challenge she'd thrown at my feet.

11

Eva

Several days after the incident in Gavin's car, I climbed the steps to the hockey arena on campus with a whole shitload of trepidation and two tickets clutched in my sweaty hand. It was at least eighty degrees outside, and I was sweating through my jeans, but the heat didn't stop me from getting in line for the free hot chocolate I was promised.

Cole had swung me two seats after my dad had cornered me with a surprise date the same night as the game. I'd known the push was coming, but I'd hoped I'd get a couple more weeks into the semester before working in Dad's required extracurriculars.

Michael Dodson, Dad's young protégé, had agreed to meet me here instead of the more traditional dinner my dad had arranged. He'd sent me a picture along with his number so we could coordinate, though both men had already agreed on Friday. My first reaction was absolutely not. Any guy willing to let my dad dictate the terms of a date without even contacting me was immediately off the list of candidates.

Not that I had a list of candidates. I didn't even have a list of hookups at this point. Gavin was the first person I'd let touch me in way too long. Maybe that was part of the problem.

I hadn't said more to Gavin than a passing hello since then. He gave me the same slow smile every time, and in my head, I heard myself brush him off after freaking out. *Thanks. I needed that.* Not my finest moment, but Gavin didn't deserve my finest moments.

Somehow, during all the grinding, I'd forgotten about his history with Kayleigh. He'd lulled me into a false sense of security with his dirty mouth and "helpful" nature. I was pissed I'd given in—and I wanted his "help" again.

I loved an orgasm as much as the next girl, but it had never been like that. Intense. Powerful. Soul shattering. He didn't even take his pants off, for fuck's sake. I drew in a slow breath as I waited for the tingles to settle down.

Why the hell was Gavin's smug confidence so hot? If any other guy talked to me the way he did, I'd lay them flat in seconds. But Gavin? I'd climbed into his lap, in broad daylight, and used him as my own personal sex toy.

I'd been in a foul mood since then, compounded by Carl sending me on some ridiculous research goose chase for his mystery project and my dad playing matchmaker. Thank God David had fixed my car the next day. Another casualty of suburban life, or in this case, the rabbits living in Gavin's neighborhood. Apparently, the wires in my car were tasty. More importantly, I'd been able to drive myself to classes and practice and this game.

The line moved and I was finally able to place my order for hot cocoa with as much whipped cream as they could fit in the cup. If nothing else, the hit of chocolate would make me less likely to attack Gavin on sight. Or my date. I needed to remember I was there to support the boys and convince my dad's choice I wasn't the one he wanted.

I followed the signs for the seat number on my ticket, and my brows went up when I realized I'd be sitting in the first row right next to TU's bench. Did they call it a bench in hockey? Damn, I needed to brush up if I was going to be doing this with any regularity.

The guys weren't out on the ice yet, but the stands were filling up fast. I'd sent Michael a pic of his ticket, which included his seat number, but that was as far as I was willing to go. If he couldn't find me, not my fault.

Music started to overtake the dull chatter of the crowd, and both hockey teams came onto the ice, skating in two big circles and taking shots at the goal. After a couple of minutes, they collected the pucks and started stretching. With nothing better to do and a lot of shit on my mind, I pulled out my phone and called Stephen. He'd at least get a kick out of this.

"Why does it look like you're at a hockey rink?" Stephen gasped as I switched to the front camera so I could focus on my four roommates, fully geared and chatting on the ice near the goal. "Dear god, are those your roommates? You are such a lucky bitch. And stingy. Where are my shower pics?"

With a sigh, I flipped the camera back. "Can you be less creepy for five seconds?"

His brows drew down as he studied my face. "What's wrong?"

I took a careful breath and smiled at him. "Nothing."

He narrowed his eyes. "Oh no you don't. That's the bullshit smile you use to hide all your big emotions."

"I'm not hiding. I'm processing." Stephen already knew about the date since I'd texted him the minute my dad had sprung it on me, but he hadn't heard the latest in the saga of Carl. "I finally got assigned something for my assistantship."

"Why aren't we more happy about this?"

"He wants me to do some vague research for a mobile A/B test group..." Stephen's eyes started to glaze over so I summed up. "It's busy work. He assigned me busy work. I wanted this spot so I could learn and get some real projects under my name. It's insulting at best."

"So quit."

I rolled my eyes. "I don't quit. Besides, even if I do no work, this assistantship can still get me seen by one of the biggest tech companies in the world. As long as I don't murder Carl before the end of the semester."

Stephen pursed his lips. "Would this company make you happy?"

"It would make my parents happy—and hopefully shift their focus away from my marriage status and onto my work."

He snorted. "You mean your status as an ice-cold player? Marriage is at least four levels away from your current booty call preferences. And I didn't hear anything about the company fulfilling you."

I sighed. "It doesn't have to be fulfilling."

Stephen shook his head. "I never thought I'd hear those words come out of *your* mouth. All summer, you couldn't stop talking about Delacourt and how much you loved it there. You had a million ideas for how to help the business grow. I'll bet a place like that doesn't give a single shit about Carl Bennington and his assistants."

"And my parents don't give a single shit about Delacourt. If I want to convince them I'm more than an accessory, I need something impressive."

Stephen leaned forward, giving me his serious face. "Making your parents proud is *not* worth your happiness."

My parents weren't the real reason I wanted this job—my brother was. A fact Stephen probably suspected, but we'd never addressed. I didn't voluntarily talk about Brendan, but tonight felt different.

I felt different. Without the bustling social life of my football crew, I felt... lost. Like I didn't know who I was anymore.

Mac and the others were busy with practices and their relationships, and I was left on the outside. None of them outright excluded me—I was still a part of the group text—but I wasn't the same as them. It was easy to push Brendan to the far reaches of my mind when I was surrounded by friends who needed help.

Less easy when Stephen was badgering me about my motivations. For once, I *wanted* to talk about him.

I pursed my lips. "What about making Brendan proud?"

His gaze fell to his lap. "It wasn't your fault."

"He'd still be alive if it weren't for me. Shouldn't I make the most of his sacrifice?"

"Yes. You should live your life for yourself—full of love and happiness and all the things he'd want for you."

Even with my sudden willingness to discuss my brother, I couldn't speak the words that went through my mind. Stephen wouldn't understand. Brendan didn't get a say in my future happiness because, according to my parents, the wrong kid had died when he'd protected me.

I blinked back the hot tears trying to form. "I'll keep that in mind. I have to go. My date will be here any minute."

Stephen tsked. "I know you're not listening right now, but at least bang the hot hockey player instead of whatever socially appropriate rich dude your dad picked out."

A laugh burst out of me. Trust Stephen to skip right to the important stuff. He knew how I felt about dealing with my own emotions. "No promises. Maybe I'll bang them both."

"Bullshit, sweet cheeks. You've been panting for the hockey player since you kissed him in the courtyard."

Since before then, but I wasn't going to admit that out loud. "I regret telling you that."

Stephen pointed at me and raised a brow. "No, you don't. Send pics. Love you."

"Love you too." I hit end just as a familiar voice spoke up from behind me.

"Good to know my brother's at least in the top two, though he's going to be pissed you brought a date to his game."

12

Eva

I spun around and came face to face with Danny King. "What are you doing here?"

He laughed. "I was invited, same as you."

"How much did you hear?"

Danny shrugged, a loose, graceful movement that reminded me of his brother. "Enough, but it's none of my business."

I checked my watch, only a couple of minutes before Michael was supposed to be here. Despite what I'd told Stephen, I had no intention of banging my dad's choice. Danny was a wild card, but I could probably use him.

"How would you feel about causing some trouble?"

His brows rose, and he gave me a slow smile. "Favorably. What do you need?"

"Come sit by me and be obnoxious to my date."

"Done." He hopped over the row separating us and took the aisle seat next to me.

Not long after Danny switched places, I spotted Michael making his way down the aisle. His neatly pressed pants and polo shirt stood out among the jeans and hoodies most of the people around him wore. Short blond hair done in the classic business style did nothing for me, and he didn't have a single visible tattoo.

When had I started counting tattoos as a turn on? I frowned as he waited with a bemused smile for a family to get their kids situated and out of the aisle. From one text message and the last fifteen seconds, he seemed like a nice enough guy. I judged it would take me less than ten minutes to convince him to leave as if it were his idea.

Michael's gaze dismissed Danny and lit up when he spotted me. "Sorry I'm late. Eva, right? I'm Michael."

"Yeah, nice to meet you. Thanks for agreeing to this instead of dinner."

"No problem." He stood awkwardly next to our row, but Danny didn't move his legs to let my date through. "Excuse me, do you mind if I squeeze past you?"

Danny tilted his head up with a lazy grin. "That depends. What are your intentions with my girl, Eva?"

Michael frowned, and I adjusted my timeline down a few minutes. "I'm sorry, who are you?"

"I'm Danny. Eva's chaperone for the evening. Gotta make sure you treat her right."

"I see." He shifted his attention to me. "Are you sure this is what you want to do? Your dad set up reservations for us in Dallas we could still make."

Danny laid his hands over his stomach, spreading a little more. "Come on, Mikey. I was only kidding. I have it on good authority you're one of the top two—"

I slapped a hand over Danny's mouth, but he kept mumbling behind my mediocre barrier. "Ignore him. He doesn't know anything. I promised my friends I'd come to the game. They were very excited."

On cue, Reece skated by the plexiglass in front of us and

blew me a kiss, followed by Cole who waved, and Gavin whose scowl implied he'd happily murder both his brother and possibly the man talking to us. When his eyes met mine, the violence melted under scorching heat. I was surprised the ice didn't start steaming.

His gaze stayed trained on me for another long beat before he turned away. Danny chuckled behind my fingers, and I quickly yanked my hand back. I wanted to fan myself —when had it gotten so hot in the arena?—but Michael caught my attention by clearing his throat.

"Look, you're very pretty, but hockey isn't really my thing. Besides, you seem busy." He nodded toward the ice. "Why don't we try this again some other night? I'll text you later."

Michael didn't wait for me to confirm before walking up the stairs to the exit. A new record thanks to Danny and my roommates. Dad's pick hadn't even lasted through warmups. I wasn't looking for a relationship, but if I was, it definitely wouldn't be with someone who bailed at the first sign of difficulty.

Danny nudged my arm. "Aren't you going to thank me for scaring him off?"

I checked to make sure Michael really was gone before responding. "No, but I'll let you buy me some nachos and sit next to me for the game."

"Now why would I want to do that?" he teased.

"Didn't you hear?" I asked in a chipper voice. "I'm very pretty."

He scrubbed a hand down his face with a laugh. "That you are. I can't wait to see you square up against Gavin. Can you let me watch?"

"No. No. I'm far too pretty to hear anything you're saying right now."

Danny's smile widened. "No wonder he's so obsessed."

I dropped the jokes and settled deeper in my chair. "He's not obsessed. He's just trying to figure out how best to keep me from murdering him before the year is out."

"Why would you murder him?"

I pursed my lips, deciding how much I wanted to share with the trouble-making twin I didn't know. My reasons weren't a secret, neither were Gavin's actions. With a mental shrug, I told him about Kayleigh.

Danny sat up and faced me, the first time he showed any inclination of caring about our conversation. "Do you mean the drunk cheerleader?"

"Yeah. I didn't realize the incident was common knowledge."

"It's not, and you don't know the whole story."

I raised a brow. "And you do?"

He gave me an amused smile. "I was there, Shortcake."

"Okay, no. I hate that nickname more than Princess."

He laughed. "You don't hate Princess."

I didn't, but I wasn't about to back down now. "I do. Gavin is an ass, and I hate the way he says it in that smug voice." Though I loved it when he whispered it in my ear right before he made me come.

Danny leaned back, tucking his hands behind his head. "Sweetheart, I'm an expert on Gavin's smug voice, and when he calls you Princess, he's staking a claim. You're *his* princess. Gavin doesn't do things halfway. He's afraid you'll use your superpowers to find out all our secrets and use them against us, but he wants you close too."

I ignored Danny's view of the situation, mostly because it tempted me to think about another round with Gavin after our one and done. "I'm not interested in your secrets unless they affect me. What do you mean you were there?"

"I was late coming into Wildcat the day your boozy friend showed up. She tripped over my foot when I held the door for her."

"At least *you* were a gentleman," I muttered.

His sly eyes slid toward me, so different from Gavin's despite looking exactly the same. "I'm no gentleman. Gavin's the one with the hero complex, not me."

I snorted out a laugh. "I find that hard to believe considering he sent my drunk friend back to her car before calling the police on her."

Danny stared down at the ice, then jerked his chin to his brother glaring up at us. "You should talk to him about it."

"Yeah, so he can spin the situation in his favor, or worse, lie to me about it."

"I won't say Gavin doesn't lie, since clearly you know about the switching, but don't you think you should have all the information before you make a decision."

The ice emptied and the stands got dark, probably signaling the beginning of the game. I chewed on my bottom lip and considered his point, ignoring Gavin's presence only a few feet from us.

"I'll consider it, but I promised Kayleigh I'd let it go."

He snorted. "So, you're as much of a liar as Gavin."

"Shut up," I muttered.

We watched the guys play for a while in relative silence. Hockey was fast paced, with the teams constantly switching out players in the middle of play. Very different from football. Danny muttered comments under his breath, until a brutal hit on Gavin made us both sit up.

"Fucking assholes. It's supposed to be an exhibition game." Danny's mouth tightened into a thin line.

I held my breath as Gavin shook his head, then let it out in a whoosh when he went right back to chasing the puck.

"They keep targeting him, though it hasn't slowed him down at all. I'm surprised he hasn't thrown down with one of them yet."

Danny draped an arm on the chair behind me and leaned closer. "Nah, he's cold on the ice. Bottles it up until he's in street clothes away from the team. If you want to see him really lose it, kiss me on the cheek during the game, then invite me up to your room after."

I raised a brow. "Is your game really that bad?"

"No. I could get the puck bunny three seats past you if I wanted to, but I like giving Gavin shit. He needs someone to shake up his life every once in a while."

"What makes you think he'll see me kiss you on the cheek?"

"Because he won't stop looking over here. If they weren't playing a team with the stick handling skills of a toddler playgroup, he'd have cost them a couple of goals."

I scanned the ice, and sure enough, Gavin passed the puck to Reece, then glanced our way. It was fast, but I caught it this time.

"No thanks. I don't see a benefit to pissing off my roommate."

"Aw, come on, Shortcake. I thought you liked to walk on the wild side."

Gavin's warning to stay away from his brother was inexorably tied to the hottest car sex of my life. I hated the idea I'd let Gavin win, even though the results had been *so good*. I'd told myself any hot guy would have done the same, but how would I know for sure unless I tested the theory?

No way was I inviting Danny into my room, but he *had* helped me with Michael—a quick kiss on the cheek didn't seem like too much to ask in return.

Before I could talk myself out of it, I leaned over to plant a chaste kiss on Danny's cheek, but at the last second, he turned his head. I should have expected the move with the way he'd been baiting me. The kiss only lasted the length of a breath before he pulled away. Long enough with his lips on mine for a test though.

No tingles. No heat. Nothing. I hadn't really expected a response, but a girl could hope. Danny was identical to Gavin, if it was simply a matter of being attracted to a hot guy, he should do it. Hell, Reece or Cole or even Mase should do it.

Nope. I sat back in my seat to the sound of Danny laughing quietly. When I absently glanced at the bench, Gavin was watching us, stone faced. A whistle blew on the ice, and Gavin turned away.

He didn't look my way again for the rest of the game, and my sense of foreboding grew at about the same rate as Danny's amusement. Whatever nonsense was happening between Gavin and me, I hoped I hadn't just taken a torch to my living arrangement.

13

Gavin

For the fourth time in an hour, a loud quack distracted me from behind the closed bathroom door. I wasn't sure if Eva was home, but Henry was in a mood today. I guess I could relate.

I wasn't pissed at the team—we'd won the exhibition game like we were supposed to—but I'd played like shit. Everyone had left me alone for the past couple of days while I stewed and pretended like I hadn't noticed Eva kiss Danny in the stands. I'd invited him as a fluke because Mase had reminded me that I did, indeed, have family that might want to come.

Danny had sent a thumbs up when I texted him, which I'd assumed meant fuck off. I hadn't considered it might mean 'I'd love to watch you play and make a move on Eva while you're fucking busy'. After watching her come all over my hand, I wasn't messing around anymore. I'd tried to keep her away from the team because I'd been worried about her causing drama, but those assholes didn't listen.

Now I wanted to keep her away from the team because

the only one fucking touching her was going to be me. Either way, the drama would be contained.

My phone buzzed from next to me on the bed, but I ignored it. I'd been in my head for days, and I had a response paper to write. I didn't have a lot of time to dedicate to schoolwork. Especially when my mind kept jumping back and forth between Danny and the date who hadn't lasted long.

Oh yeah, I knew about the date. Cole said Eva had been set up by her dad, and I'd had no doubt Eva could handle the blond guy in the polo who'd stopped to talk to her. I wasn't so sure about my brother.

Two more messages came in on my phone, pulling my thoughts from Eva. Again. Dammit. This was exactly why I hadn't wanted her getting involved with anyone on the team. She fucks with their heads. I shoved the book away and checked my notifications to see a couple of messages from Carter, getting progressively more dramatic.

> Carter: I'm in town. Let's have lunch.
>
> Carter: Stop ignoring me.
>
> Carter: Fine. I'll eat lunch by myself.
>
> Carter: [sad face emoji]
>
> Me: What are you doing in town?
>
> Carter: Passing through.
>
> Me: Can't. Studying for a test.

Almost immediately, my phone rang. I rolled my eyes. Carter didn't give a shit about my grades as long as I was eligible to play. With a sigh, I closed the textbook and answered the phone.

"I can't study if I'm talking to you either."

Carter laughed, and the sound of traffic filtered in behind him. "I'll be quick. Have you heard the latest from Dallas?"

I leaned back against the headboard and ran a hand through my hair. "No. They've been hands off for a while."

He snorted. "Yeah, because they've been courting Boilard, a new right winger from the CHL."

I cursed quietly, trying not to assume the worst.

"Don't worry, kid. I have it on good authority they still want you, but they also want to have options depending on how this year goes."

My teeth ground together as my jaw clenched. I'd done everything right, and I still might lose my shot because of a stupid mistake three years ago. None of the other teams showed any interest after the shit hit the fan, so if Dallas passed on me, going undrafted free agent likely wasn't going to get me anything else.

"What can I do?" I ground out.

"Play the way you did before you got scared."

I wasn't scared—I was careful. Carter knew that. I'd earned the bad boy reputation from one incident, and Dallas had been very clear about my supposedly reckless attitude. With their warning in mind, I'd adjusted my playstyle to avoid penalties at all costs. Not good enough apparently.

"I'm the leading scorer on our team, and I have the least penalty minutes. What more do they want?"

"A championship would be nice, but they want more than technical skill. Boilard is creative in making plays happen and taking advantage of the other team's mistakes. You're better than him—I've seen it—but you need to prove it to Dallas."

"Sure. No problem," I muttered.

Carter hesitated. "Gavin, I'm going to tell you this as a friend, not as an agent. You have options outside the team that drafted you. I know it seems like you don't, but if Dallas passes, your career's not over."

Since I was playing in college, I wasn't allowed to officially have an agent, which meant I couldn't officially shop around to see if there was interest from another team. Technically, I probably shouldn't even be talking to Carter, but he'd been friends with my dad before my parents died.

When I didn't respond, Carter sighed. "If this is about Danny—"

I cut him off before he could ask me about my brother. "I'll keep that in mind. Thanks, man."

He grunted, and I hung up the phone. Another quack came from the bathroom, and I gave up on studying.

I'd been busy with the semester ramping up and trying to get in some extra ice time to prep for the showdown with Easton, so I hadn't seen Eva or Henry in a few days. Admittedly, I didn't know much about ducks, but Henry sounded annoyed.

After Carter's pep talk, I could use a distraction.

When I opened the bathroom door, the duck chattered up at me. She was curled up in a sweatshirt wearing her usual colorful diaper. The rest of the bathroom was empty. I stepped over her and peered through Eva's open door. Clothes covered her bed and soft music played from somewhere inside.

I came into the room ready to start a fight to relieve some of my tension, but I found her sitting at her desk with her head buried in her arms.

"Eva?"

She immediately popped up and smoothed down the

figure-hugging lines of her bold red dress. "What are you doing in here?"

The weary note in her voice triggered all kinds of protective instincts I thought I'd buried years ago. Eva did not need my protection. She was more than capable of eviscerating her enemies without my help.

I nodded at the door I'd just come through. "Why is Henry hiding on my side of the bathroom?"

"I wasn't aware we had sides of the bathroom." She dismissed me and turned to the mirror she'd propped in the corner.

I held out my hands. "I was just checking to be sure your duck was okay."

"Why does it matter? You don't care." She sounded tired and sad, which was apparently my weakness because the truth slipped out before I could stop it.

"Yes, I do." Her gaze whipped around to me, and I shrugged. We probably should have had this conversation after the car. Might as well go all the way. "I care about Henry, and I care about you."

Eva's lips parted as she stared at me. "What?"

"I'm not the monster you seem to think I am."

Her brows came together, and she studied me for a long beat. Her mouth opened like she was going to ask another question, then she closed it again with a shake of her head.

"I don't think you're a monster."

"Oh, so now we're lying to each other?"

Her lips tipped up. "Okay, I *did* think you were an asshole, but I've recently considered it might not be malicious."

"Did?"

"Good point, that should have been in present tense since I still think you're an asshole."

Some of the fire had returned to her eyes, but I didn't like the way she kept tugging on her dress as if she were nervous. The Eva I knew didn't get nervous.

I crossed my arms and leaned against the doorframe. "You okay, Princess? Someone disobey a royal order?"

She set her phone on the desk and turned toward me. "I don't have time to battle with you right now. Henry's okay. She's pouting because I'm going out and your door is closed."

"Why didn't you ask me to open it?"

"Henry isn't your responsibility. She's fine on her own for a few hours."

Eva turned back to her mirror, her dress riding high on her thighs, and I jerked my eyes back up to her face. As much as I wanted the freedom to look, she didn't need me ogling her when she was clearly upset about something.

"You don't sound too happy to be going out."

"I'll work on that," she muttered, tugging on the damn dress again and peeking at her phone on the desk.

What was it about this girl that slipped past all my defenses? There was something about her vulnerability that split me open. I'd assumed Eva was a spoiled, entitled brat, but I'd been wrong. Or mostly wrong. Eva *was* a brat. She teased and taunted and refused to give an inch unless she was in charge.

But she wasn't spoiled or entitled. She cleaned and arranged food and took care of all of us without complaint. I'd seen how hard she worked at cheer practice, and I'd witnessed the risks she took to be the best at her sport. She loved Henry—more than her own comfort—and like the day in the courtyard, I couldn't stand to see her upset.

I came fully into the room. "You going to tell me what's wrong?"

Her head dropped for a second, and when she looked up, she'd donned her smile like armor. "I'm fine. You can go back to whatever you were doing before Henry bothered you."

Eva expected me to leave, but her smile was still brittle on the edges and her knuckles were white where she gripped her desk chair. The similarities between this moment and the day in the courtyard weren't lost on me.

I shook my head and moved closer. "You can push everyone else away with the happy act, but not me. Might as well tell me what's wrong since I'm not going back to my room until you do."

She studied my face, then her shoulders dipped, and she sank onto the edge of her bed. "It's not an act. I *am* fine. Most days."

"But not today."

Eva took a shuddering breath and stared down at her hands. "Not today. Can we do this some other time?"

Her quiet request had the opposite effect. No way would I leave her to deal with whatever it was alone. I sat beside her, not quite touching, and reached for the hands she was tangling together.

"Talk to me."

"Why do you think I'd trust you enough to talk about something serious?"

"Because you trusted me enough to let me get you off in a car in broad daylight outside your cheer practice."

She scoffed. "Maybe that's just a normal Tuesday for me and you were the lucky winner."

"It's not, but I'll give you the lucky part. How about this... you already think we hate each other—whatever you tell me couldn't make things worse. If I was going to spread your secrets, I already have plenty of fodder."

Eva gave a half-assed tug on her hand, but I held tight. "I can't like you. It messes with my world view."

"You don't have to like me to talk."

She let out a quiet breath, and I knew I'd won. "Sixteen years ago today, my brother died saving my life."

14

Eva

Gavin's hand was warm in mine, and his weight on the mattress pulled me toward him. Or maybe it was him. I was so *tired* of fighting. The small amount of effort I needed to keep myself upright and away from him seemed like too much.

If I let myself, I could simply give in. Tumble against his shoulder, into his lap—let him catch me when I couldn't hold myself up. For a long second, I could imagine it. Tempting, but not worth the risk.

I tugged again, and he still wouldn't let me go. Figured. I could control everyone except the one man I despised. His words circled in my mind. *You already think we hate each other.* Except I was fairly certain I didn't hate him.

Danny—and okay, Gavin himself—had made me question my absolute conviction of Gavin's role as villain. He goaded me, taunted me, challenged me, and in my weak moments like now, he refused to let me wallow on my own. I really should take Danny's advice to ask him about Kayleigh, but I couldn't handle another conversation where I needed to dig for the truth. Not today.

"I'm sorry," Gavin murmured, but he made no move to leave.

I swallowed and adjusted my stupid dress again, trying to get the clingy material to cover more than the bare minimum. "I hate today. Every year, I consider locking my door and sleeping through it, but I can't. Brendan would give me so much shit if I gave up like that."

Gavin's thumb stroked my wrist, sending goosebumps up my arm. "It's not giving up to take time for yourself."

Stephen had told me the same thing the one time we discussed it, but they didn't understand. Today wasn't about me. Today was one of the few days when I didn't silence the memories. I hadn't tried to explain it to Stephen, but Gavin sat next to me, patiently waiting while I sorted through my thoughts.

"No one warns you the world moves on. My friends move on. My parents move on. I'm the only one still here missing him." A tear slipped out despite my best intentions, hitting my thigh with a warm splat.

"Tell me about him."

"Why?" I sniffled, trying desperately to keep the rest of the tears at bay.

"So you won't be the only one missing him today."

I clenched my eyes closed, but it was too late. His sincere tone broke through the thin wall holding back the torrent. My chest constricted with the pressure of trying to keep myself together, and I shook with silent sobs.

Gavin shifted his grip from my hand to the back of my head, pulling me against him while I tried to suck in air. His arms came around me, and I clung to him, soaking his shirt while I bawled. At some point, he scooted us back on the bed to lean on the headboard with me in his lap.

"It's okay. I've got you," he whispered into my hair.

My dress hiked up, but I barely noticed. He was warm, so warm, and I hadn't cried like this in years. I let go. I let all the shame and anger and sadness flow through me without trying to wrestle them into submission.

And Gavin held me through it all.

Once I calmed down enough to take normal breaths, I told him the first thing I always remembered about Brendan. "He was fearless except for spiders. Hated them. I used to make little pipe cleaner spiders and hide them in his bed. When I was scared, *I* used to hide in his bed. We'd spend hours under the covers with him telling me stories about horses."

Gavin tilted his head to look down at me. "Horses?"

"I wanted to own a horse farm for sad horses when I grew up, so I could make them happy again."

He chuckled above me. "And now you adopt ducks instead."

"Just one duck, but Brendan would have loved Henry. He was six years older than me, but he was my best friend."

"How did he save your life?"

I tucked my face against Gavin's neck, riding out the usual guilt. Most people assumed he'd given me an organ or something equally noble, but no. Brendan died from my stubbornness.

"Did anyone tell you about the really bad storms that tore through central Texas sixteen years ago?"

He gave a single head shake. "I grew up in Ohio, and if it wasn't related to hockey, I probably didn't notice."

"My parents sent me and my brother to this exclusive private school. Preschool through graduation with the same rich people. I was in kindergarten, at recess playing some castle game where I told my friends what job they'd have in my court."

Gavin gave a short laugh as he combed his fingers through my hair. "Sounds about right."

"They'd warned us if the storm hit, we'd have to switch to indoor quiet time in the gym. I hated quiet time because all the kids were stuffed in there together doing what the teachers wanted. When the sirens went off, I wasn't done creating my kingdom. The teachers came around collecting everyone, but I crawled under the slide and hid."

My voice broke, and his hand trailed down my hair to stroke my back. "Breathe, Eva."

I took a couple of slow, deep breaths until I had control of my vocal cords again. "Brendan couldn't see me with my class in the gym, so he snuck outside. I was crying when he found me. Big angry clouds blocked out the sun, and the wind had pulled the bow out of my hair. I refused to come out from under the slide, so he wedged himself in behind me, curling around my back. I don't remember the tornado or how close it came, but I *do* remember the crack of the play structure breaking."

The sound haunted me.

"I woke up in the hospital and called for Brendan. My parents left the room. I didn't understand what had happened. I cried and screamed for my brother until one of the nurses got up the lady balls to tell me why I couldn't have him. My twelve-year-old brother had shielded me from the playground collapsing. I had a minor concussion from hitting my head on the slide, but no other injuries. He died."

Gavin's chest rose and fell under my cheek, and I focused on the steady rhythm. The chaos of my emotions settled, and for once, I felt lighter.

"I know nothing I say will fix it, but I'm glad you had those years with your brother where you knew, absolutely, he loved you. That's what I remind myself when things get dark."

I remembered his comment from our fateful day in the courtyard. "Your mom?"

"Both my parents died my senior year of high school. I'd already been drafted by Dallas, and Danny and I were playing hockey on the other side of the state with the USHL. They were driving to one of our games when they were hit by a drunk driver."

"I'm sorry," I whispered, hurting for him.

He blew out a breath. "It sucked. So much. If I hadn't pushed to be the best, play at the highest level, we'd have been at a local high school and my parents wouldn't have been on that road."

"If you hadn't pushed, you wouldn't be one of the best college hockey players and on the verge of playing professionally in Dallas. You wouldn't be here."

"Neither would you."

We lay together, connected by our losses, and the paths that led to this moment. Gavin *did* understand. Actions could have disastrous consequences.

"Have you talked to your parents about today?" he asked.

I let out a dry laugh. "We don't talk about Brendan. Family rule. My dad *did* call earlier, and I made the mistake of answering. He has another potential suitor for me."

Gavin tensed up, very slightly, and let me change the subject. "Why are you letting your dad set you up?"

"How much did Cole tell you about the guy at the game?"

His gaze cut to me, and I could practically see him moving past the part where I kissed his brother. "He said you needed a second ticket for a date."

"I agreed to go on dates with guys of my dad's choosing in exchange for them paying for my final year of college."

"Why does he care who you date?"

"It's more about who I'm not dating. His campaign manager dug up the pic of me and Mac kissing, and he lost it. He's never liked Mac, and according to him, scholarship athletes shouldn't be worth my time."

Gavin chuckled. "If he could only see you now."

I dug my finger into his side, a futile exercise because it was like trying to poke a rock, but otherwise, I didn't move. "You and I aren't dating."

The silence stretched for a beat, two, then, "What if we were?"

"Gavin, I don't date. For a lot of reasons, but in this case, I can't afford for my dad to think I'm breaking our agreement."

"What about the guy tonight?"

"I'll spend a few hours with him at a party, thank him politely for a nice time no matter how not nice it ends up being, and come back here alone."

His hand trailed down my side to the hem of my scrunched-up dress. "If you're coming home alone, why the sexy dress?"

"I have a reputation to uphold. Can't be intimidating if I show up to a frat party in sweats. Besides, what if he's cute and I change my mind?"

Gavin's fingertip grazed the bare skin of my thigh, and I stopped moving. Shadows had darkened the room while we talked, warning me I was running out of time, but I didn't want to move. I wanted to see if Gavin's hand felt as good a second time.

"Is that all it takes to change your mind?" He dipped

under the material, and my inner muscles squeezed at his teasing tone.

"Sometimes." I forced myself to think with my head instead of my vagina and tacked on a warning. "With cute roommates it takes a little more. As a rule, the dick isn't worth the mess."

He brushed his lips over my hair and moved his hand back to safer territory. "My dick has nothing to do with whether or not you live here. When do you need to leave?"

With his hand on my back again, I fought off disappointment that he'd taken my warning seriously. "Soon. I still need to do my makeup and find my shoes."

Gavin nodded, catching a few strands of my hair with his stubble. "Guess I'd better go then."

My hand clenched the material of his shirt as I fought the urge to ask him to stay. He didn't move me on his own, and I knew he wouldn't. Gavin was giving me the choice.

I hesitated.

In the stillness, Henry's quack echoed off the bathroom walls, and I remembered my actions had consequences. If I blew off the date, I could be sacrificing everything I'd worked for up to this point.

I let go of his shirt and slid off his lap, adjusting my dress as I stood. "Thank you."

His dark eyes followed me back to the mirror before he rolled off the bed himself. "Be careful tonight."

I didn't watch him leave. The knot in my stomach said I'd made the wrong choice, picking a blind date over my roommate, but Gavin was still the bigger wild card. Getting involved with him could come with so many problems if feelings got involved. I'd learned that lesson the hard way with Mac.

If I needed a release, I could always find someone at the party once I played the role of dutiful daughter. I ignored the voice laughing at me in the back of my mind and grabbed my makeup case to start repairing the damage I'd done when I'd let Gavin past my defenses.

15

Gavin

Leaving Eva's room after she'd hesitated was one of the hardest things I'd ever done. I hadn't planned to float the idea of dating, but I didn't regret the words—only the outcome. She'd nearly killed me when she broke down, and I wanted to be the one to make sure she never felt alone again.

I waited until Eva left in her Uber to text the guys. Reece would know where the frat party was happening tonight. As hockey players, we had a standing invite to all parties, but the few I'd attended hadn't seemed worth the energy. Until now.

> Me: Reece, where's the party tonight?
>
> Reece: Whaaat? You in?
>
> Cole: Since when do you go to parties?
>
> Mase: h8 u all. muting chat
>
> Me: We're all going. Where?
>
> Reece: Kappa house

I groaned, and Henry waddled out of the bathroom door I'd left open for her. Kappa parties were notorious for trouble. A bunch of business bros who thought money meant they could be assholes. Any guy who thought a Kappa party made a good first date wasn't looking for a relationship, no matter what her dad said.

I had to remind myself the Eva everyone else knew wasn't the one crying in my arms earlier. She knew her way around parties and business bros. I had to respect her choice, meaning I'd follow her to the party and refrain from beating the shit out of her date as long as she looked like she was having a good time.

Henry chittered at me, so I picked her up right as Reece burst through my door.

"No. We're not bringing the duck. I love Henry, but I haven't sampled the puck bunny wares in way too long."

Cole appeared next to him. "Are you crashing Eva's date?"

I frowned. "We're not crashing anything. I just don't trust Eva's date to keep his hands off her."

Reece raised a brow. "What makes you think Eva doesn't want his hands on her?"

The way she'd let me hold her. The hitch in her breathing when I'd brushed a kiss on her head. The slight scrape of her nails against my stomach when I'd slipped my finger under her skirt.

My jaw clenched at the thought of some other guy's hands on her thigh. "Trust me. I'm helping."

Cole took Henry from me and shook his head sadly. "Don't worry. I'm sure when Eva's done with you she'll hand your balls back mostly intact."

Reece made a horrified expression. "Remind me to *never* ask for your help with the ladies."

Mase popped his head around the corner. "What's with the secret meeting?"

"If you hadn't muted chat, you'd know," Reece taunted him.

Sometimes I hated my roommates. "Can we focus please?"

Reece filled him in, adding, "It's about time Gavin had some fun."

I pinched the bridge of my nose. "We're only going for Eva."

He snorted. "Maybe you are. I'm going to find a nice lady to spend some quality naked time with."

Mase shoved his hands in the pockets of his jeans. "I'll go too. That way when Eva kicks your ass for following her and you drown your sorrows in cheap whiskey, I can drive you home."

All three of us turned to stare at him, but his expression didn't change. As usual, I couldn't tell if he was joking. "Okay, Cole?"

He shook his head. "Nah, I'll stay with Henry if you guys want to go out. You know how she gets cranky when left alone. We have an episode of Next Best Ninja to watch anyway."

I was pretty sure *Cole* wasn't joking, which made the whole conversation even weirder. "Fine, Cole is on duck duty. Mase is DD. Reece is a manwhore as usual. Can you at least control your baser instincts long enough for us to determine if we need to flatten Eva's date?"

"Of course, anything for Eva. Did you know she got me a box of condoms the last time she had groceries delivered? If you weren't basically tattooing your name on her ass, she might be my dream girl."

"Great. Let's go."

We all piled into my car, except Cole who waved from the door, and I drove us to Kappa house in the money part of town. As expected, the place was full. On a warm night like tonight, there were usually girls in bikini tops and shorts covering the lawn in small groups.

Instead, we found a dressier event with an alumni banner draped over the door. No wonder Eva had pulled out the red dress. The plastic cups had been replaced with wine glasses, and I had the first inkling I may have been in over my head.

I parked on the street, and the three of us stood on the sidewalk watching people in cocktail attire mingle on the porch. We were dressed in jeans and shirts, so at least we weren't rocking the hobo athlete look, but we definitely didn't fit in.

I didn't give a fuck.

Inside, the party edged closer to what I'd expected. Loud music, plenty of liquor, and a packed dance floor in the middle of the living room. Either the older alumni had left, or they were busy reliving their youths among the jumble of drunk frat guys.

Reece rubbed his hands together and scanned the room, while Mase took up position on the wall next to the door. A group of girls slowed as they passed by, smiling at us. Reece smiled back, but I swear Mase growled at them.

"Do you see Eva?" I asked them.

Reece popped one shoulder up. "No, but to be fair I'm not looking for her either."

Mase shook his head. "Go find her. I'll wait here."

"Good plan." Reece slapped my back and wandered into the crowd.

I didn't mind. If I needed backup, he'd be there, like always.

Reece, Mase, and I were all several inches taller than most of the people in the room, but I didn't see a dark red dress or a pink-streaked blonde head anywhere. I pushed through the dancers grinding all over each other and made my way into the second big space with a huge table in the middle of the room. A bar had been set up on a long side table, with the wine glasses, which I now realized were plastic, stacked on one corner.

Eva stood at the other corner with her hip cocked, smiling politely at a guy in a dark blue blazer. He gestured wildly with his cup, clear plastic instead of the classic red, and she had to sidestep his arm. Liquid sloshed over the edge of his cup, and he swayed a little as he overcorrected. Probably drunk. Definitely not a match for Eva.

I did my best impression of Mase and tried to blend into the woodwork. Until the guy's hand curled around Eva's hip. I couldn't tell if he was trying to pull her closer or just grab her ass at an awkward angle, but it didn't matter—I was already moving.

Eva stepped out of his reach, smoothly shifting his hand to the back of a chair next to them, then frowned as she noticed me. "Gavin?"

Her date swung around, swayed again, and tried to throw an arm around Eva's waist. I stepped between them, and he got an armload of me instead. With a start, he backed up, running into the table.

"Sorry," he mumbled to the furniture.

I shook my head. What had her dad been thinking? This idiot was probably the son of a frat brother or something. Eva sidled up next to me with a quiet sigh. I knew how hard today was for her, and she'd been dealing with this guy for most of the evening. My patience for him quickly depleted as I caught him checking out her cleavage. Time to close things out.

I met her gaze and nodded at her date. "You going to politely thank him for a nice evening?"

Her eyes threatened retribution, but she smiled at him. "It was nice meeting you, Shawn."

His brows dropped. "I thought we could go—"

Eva's smile turned lethal. "No, and you might want to rethink treating your date like a Tinder hookup the next time it's set up by her father."

He looked like he was going to argue, but even drunk, he seemed to think better of it when I stepped in front of her.

As expected, Reece showed up exactly when I needed him, clapping an arm around Shawn's shoulders. "Why don't we take a walk, yeah?"

The guy squinted up at him. "Do I know you?"

Reece showed his teeth in a sharp smile. "Doesn't everyone? Star center for Wildcat hockey? Stud on and off the ice?"

When the guy just stared at him blankly, Reece patted his chest. "Don't worry. We have plenty of time to get to know each other."

As he forcibly walked Shawn away, he raised a brow at me, asking if I needed him for anything else. I shook my head. We probably wouldn't see him again until dawn. I didn't care as long as he showed up on time for morning skate. Now that we'd cleared the way, I had a point to prove with my beautiful, stubborn roommate.

I leaned down to Eva. "I thought you were looking for a Tinder hookup."

"Not at the behest of my father." She squared up and crossed her arms over her chest. "I don't need you getting rid of my dates for me."

"Don't worry. Reece will make sure he sleeps it off somewhere safe."

"And what am I supposed to do when he reports back to my dad that some hulking hockey player interrupted our date?"

"He's so trashed he won't remember what happened. You can make up whatever story you like." I didn't bother trying to hide the bite in my tone.

"You're the one fucking with my life—you don't get to be upset right now." She pushed past me, making it to the archway leading to the kitchen before I blocked her.

The dining room had emptied, but the kitchen was full of people, so I lowered my voice. "Like hell, I don't. You let him touch you."

Eva's chin lifted as she glared at me. "I let *you* touch me. He tried and failed to grab my ass all on his own." She shoved against my chest, but I caught her wrists, holding her there.

"As I remember it, you decided run off with that guy instead of letting me touch you."

She huffed. "That doesn't mean I was going anywhere alone with him."

"Not cute enough for your tastes?"

Instead of struggling, she flattened her hands and stepped closer. "I guess I'm looking for something a little messier."

The air vibrated with her words, and I couldn't look away. A challenge passed between us—a blurred line we hadn't crossed yet—but then she pulled her wrists out of my loosened grip.

"My date's over, but I'm not ready to go yet. I'll see you later."

My brows flew up. "You're still looking for a hookup?"

"A girl's got needs."

"Princess, I know all about your needs, but you're not satisfying them here."

Her jaw firmed. "I'm not going home."

"Fine."

I tossed her pouty ass over my shoulder, making sure the bottom hem of her dress stayed in place without her flashing anyone. Eva locked her legs together, and I had to resist the urge to lick the flexed thigh muscle next to my face.

If she wasn't going home, I was the *only* one who'd be taking care of her needs. She wanted a hookup, so I'd give it to her—complete with an asshole exit strategy. Hopefully, I'd prove she was looking for a lot more.

The pulsing beat of the music in the living room matched the pounding in my blood as I crossed the room. Mase raised a brow when I passed him, but no one else seemed to notice I was carrying their campus queen to the first empty room I could find.

"Gavin, put me down," she hissed at my ass.

For a second, I wondered if she might bite me, but the joke was on her. I liked that shit.

"Gavin." Her tone was getting frostier by the second, but she couldn't wiggle without losing half her outfit.

I skipped the stairs in favor of a long, dark hallway. The Kappas looked like they'd left the lights off to discourage people from coming this way. Good. The first door I tried was a linen closet. Not big enough for my purposes. The second door was some kind of study. Shelves lined the walls stacked with thick books I'd bet no one used.

Perfect.

I set her on her feet, and she immediately went for the fancy bar cart in the corner. The glasses in here were real, and the liquor was probably meant for impressing rich alumni. Eva poured two fingers of amber liquid and held up the glass in a toast.

"Fuck men." She tossed back the expensive whiskey as if it were a shot of Fireball. "Next time I'm going straight for the alcohol instead of sipping water all night."

Eva set the glass down and wandered toward me, trailing her fingers along the desk then the bookshelves. She stopped about a foot away and spread her arms. "What's your plan here, Gavin? Keep me away from all the dangerous orgasms at the party?"

"No." I moved toward her, gratified when she held her ground. "I'm planning to keep all the dangerous orgasms in here."

"What are you saying?" she rasped.

I ran my fingers under her dress and slowly dragged my hand up, the way I'd wanted to do earlier. "You want to get off? Use me."

She eyed the door as I inched the material higher. "All I have to do is say stop and you'd be hands off."

"I would, but you're not going to ask me to stop."

Her voice deepened, turned breathy. "There's nothing preventing me from walking right out that door and going back to the party."

"Don't tempt me, Princess. I have no problem fucking you against the wall out there." I dipped my head, breathing in the spicy scent along her neck. "Is that what you want? For everyone to see the way you come apart for me?"

Her chest heaved, and she licked her lips. "This doesn't go past tonight."

With her dress around her waist, I palmed her ass and squeezed. "I don't make promises I won't keep."

"Fine," she breathed.

Ice Cold Player

If she was looking for a meaningless hookup, I'd give her what she wanted. For now. I backed Eva against the wall hard enough to knock a couple of books loose. She reached for my pants, but I grabbed both wrists and held them above her head.

"You want to come? You're going to ask nicely."

"Dammit, Gavin."

I grinned and swiped my tongue along her neck just under her ear. "Wrong answer."

She gasped when I lifted her and turned, setting her bare ass on the desk. I eased her thong down her legs, then stuck it in my pocket. "Spread for me. Let me see that pretty pussy."

Eva bit her lip as she leaned back and gave me access.

I teased her by trailing my hands all the way up, then circling back down. When she gave a frustrated grunt, I drew my thumb through her slit, brushing her clit on the way up, then backed away. Her muscles flexed as she tried to close her legs, but I held them open, preventing her from having any relief.

She whimpered, and her hands closed into fists on the desk. I made it my mission to torture her with pleasure. Taking her mouth to swallow the curses she threw at me while I played. Eva was so responsive it didn't take me long to figure out what she loved, what made her squeeze me tight with her thighs.

Her body pulled taut, and I eased her back, kissing my way down her stomach. Eva trembled under me as I got my first taste of her, but I only brought her to the edge, not enough to push her over. Not when I wanted her surrender first.

"Please, Gavin," she begged.

She was soaking wet for me as I slid two fingers into her. "Fuck yes, baby."

Her back arched with a loud moan, exactly what I wanted to hear. I worked her clit with my tongue, in a rhythm with my hand, and her hips rose to meet me. For the second time, I watched Eva come with my name on her lips.

She panted, looking down at me, and I met those ice blue eyes as I licked my fingers clean. I loved her taste, and if I had my way, I could do this every day. But she didn't want that. Eva leaned toward me, and I couldn't resist kissing her again. A slow tease of lips and breath and tongue. The soft moment nearly made me change my mind, but I had bigger plans than simply getting her off.

I'd put the pink flush there, the dazed look in her eyes, and I wanted her to think of me the next time she had the urge to find someone for her needs.

She sighed as I eased away. I helped her off the desk and straightened her dress, but I didn't give her underwear back. Instead, I tilted her head up with a finger under her chin. "Mase is waiting outside to take you home when you're ready. Enjoy the party."

The hardest part of my plan was walking away from her, but I didn't look back. She wanted a random fuck. No one in that house would question that's what she'd gotten.

16

Eva

Fuck men, fuck bacon grease, and fuck Gavin in particular. I blew hair out of my face as I scrubbed a pan with meat chunks melded to the metal. No wait, I was actively *not* fucking Gavin. Not after he walked out last night then had the audacity to not come home.

I'd waited. After the library, after finding Mase, after cuddling with Henry and questioning my life choices—I'd waited on his bed until I'd fallen asleep.

When I'd woken up this morning alone, the guys had already made breakfast and left for morning skate. Mase had left me a short note next to a plate of food. Their first real game was tonight, and Gavin had crashed with a friend.

Cole had mentioned the game already, and I'd even considered going again if I could get tickets, but Stephen had cleared his schedule to come up for a three-day weekend. He knew what the date meant.

I was excited to see him later this afternoon, especially because I needed a good bitch session about my infuriating roommate and my useless assistantship. Carl had emailed me this morning with another set of busy work tasks.

The bacon finally came off the pan, and I rinsed away the rest of the soap. Cleaning up after them wasn't too bad in most cases, but bacon was a bitch. I'd also give several years of my life to never have to scrub a toilet again. Why were men so disgusting when they could literally aim when they peed?

The door closed as I was setting the last bowls in the dishwasher, and I didn't have to turn around to figure out who'd come in. The zip down my spine told me all I needed to know. Plus, Henry had a special welcome quack for Gavin, and she'd been stewing right along with me last night.

"Hey, baby girl," Gavin murmured, dropping his bag with a thud.

Henry's feet thwapped the hardwood floor as she ran over to him. Traitor. I took my time drying off my hands, then turned and leaned against the laminate countertop. Gavin picked up my duck and held her in one hand while she fluffed her feathers at him.

He shifted his eyes from her to me. "Eva."

I refused to acknowledge the heat in my belly. Just like I'd *never* admit it, but I preferred 'Princess'. "Gavin."

He was wearing different clothes from last night, sweats and an underlayer shirt, and his hair was wet, probably from a shower. It was tempting to assume he'd been with another girl last night. After all, 'a friend' was almost always code for a hookup. I could pretend he was the kind of asshole who left one girl and immediately picked up another, but if Gavin had wanted sex, he could have had it last night.

After losing it yesterday afternoon, I'd gone looking for something to distract me, and I'd found it. Despite what I'd implied to Gavin, I hadn't wanted a random hookup, which was why I'd stayed so long with my drunk-ass date. It killed me to admit it, but I'd wanted Gavin.

When he showed up, I couldn't handle the truth, so I lied. To myself and to him. He'd given me exactly what I'd asked for, and it hadn't been enough. Now I was pissed at myself as much as him. I was self-aware enough to recognize I'd lost control a while ago, and the easiest way to wrest it back was to shove Gavin safely into the role I'd assigned him.

The problem was I couldn't make myself believe it. This time, not even the knowledge of what he'd done—allegedly done—to Kayleigh swayed me. Still, it would have been nice for him to come *talk* to me after stealing my third favorite thong and making me question the skills of every guy who'd ever touched me.

Gavin set Henry on the floor then stretched his arms over his head, causing his shirt to ride up and reveal the deep V of muscle on his lower abs. Jesus.

I crossed my arms and glared at him. "Do you guys have to make bacon *every* morning?"

He laughed and started toward the stairs. "I'm too tired for this. I'm going to go take a nap."

"If you're so tired, maybe you should have come home last night." What the hell was I doing pushing him? He'd made his position perfectly clear. Get off and get out. Except I'd been the only one to get off. As far as I knew.

Fuck.

Gavin paused with his hand on the newel post. He lowered his head for a long second, then turned back toward me. The dark amusement in his eyes surprised me, and I had a sudden carnal memory of his breath against my ear as he pinned me to a bookshelf.

"Did you miss me, Princess?"

The nickname hit me like a caress, and I cursed myself for the weakness. For last night. For the afternoon in the car. For agreeing to his deal in the first place. Gavin was a weakness, and I needed to find a way to shore up my defenses.

"I want my thong back."

He ambled closer, pursing his lips and pretending to consider my demand. "What do I get for it?"

I narrowed my eyes, pushing past the thrum of danger in his predatory gait. "You get the ability to show up for your game tonight without an ice skate shoved up your ass."

Fire lit in his eyes, and he leaned down to whisper in my ear. "Wrong answer."

My pulse picked up, and I fought to keep my breathing even. Damn him and damn my stupid involuntary reactions to him.

With my vulnerable side exposed, I lashed out. "You want to keep my underwear as a trophy? Fine—I have plenty—but I was right. This is messy. I have a lot going on right now, always, and I have neither the time nor the inclination for anything more than casual."

"That's not what you want," he challenged me.

"You don't know anything about what I want," I lied.

"I know what you don't want—the men your dad is dangling in front of you, your friend Mac, a random hookup, literally any of the guys on campus who'd give their right ball for a smile from you. You could pick any one of them, and they'd be naked and willing in seconds. You're pissed because I'm the one you want. You're just too afraid to admit it."

"Oh, I'll admit it. You're sexy as fuck, and I'd bone down in a second if I didn't think it would end with one of us murdering the other." I held up a finger. "And to be clear, I'm the one murdering you in this scenario."

He crossed his arms. "You wish you could take me."

"Regardless. I would clearly enjoy a sexual relationship with you, but you're not special. Which I'd have told you last night if you'd come home."

He raised a brow. "You're angry at me for not coming home so you could tell me yesterday meant nothing?"

I couldn't bring myself to agree with him, even though staying silent weakened my position. Yesterday hadn't meant nothing. Gavin had given me a place to fall apart, and he'd shared some of his own rough past. My goal wasn't to belittle the connection, but to get him to understand it couldn't go anywhere.

When I didn't answer, he nodded slowly, trailing his hand down my arm to link our fingers. "You don't have to try to push me away—it won't work anyway. I'm not going anywhere. Neither are you because as much as you may deny it, you know I'm right."

"Also because we both live here," I muttered. "Roommates with benefits never works out."

I was getting creative with the truth. Most of my friends had lived with their significant others before committing. The disbelieving look Gavin gave me said he knew at least a little about my previous social group.

"I'm not talking about roommates with benefits. I'm talking about you and me and a connection neither of us expected."

"The only connection we have is a bathroom. You don't know me at all."

He drew me closer, slowly, like he was dealing with a wild animal. "I know you better than you think I do, and I can prove it."

I'd been right earlier. Gavin was dangerous. I should walk away, but I didn't move. "How?"

"A bet—to show I'm more than a convenient set of fingers."

"And tongue," I added. "Can't forget the phenomenal tongue work."

He offered me a smirk. "Oh, I haven't forgotten."

I bit the inside of my cheek. "What are your terms?"

"I bet I can make you blush during my game."

"That's going to be hard since I'm not going to your game."

"Afraid you might lose?"

"I don't lose, and I have plans with another guy." Technically, I was spending time with Stephen.

His brows flew up. "Another date already?"

I shrugged, letting him believe what he wanted.

Gavin's confidence didn't lessen one iota. "Bring him. I can get two tickets. He'll just help me demonstrate my point." He stroked a finger down my cheek. "You won't let anyone else affect you, but you'll blush for me."

The petty part of me wanted to prove him wrong so badly, to punish him for making me want more. I could do it. Nothing embarrassed me, and Stephen liked the sport of hockey almost as much as the hockey players. He was coming with me to the football game on Saturday, but tonight was free.

"What do I get when I win?"

He rubbed his jaw. "You can hire a cleaning service."

Hope shot through me, a cruel reminder he really did know my weaknesses. "And if by some miracle you win?"

"Then you go on a date with me."

I scoffed. "If this is about getting laid, you had a better shot last night."

He raised my hand to kiss my wrist. "I don't want roommates with benefits. Sex is easy. I want the messy version where you come to me when you're sad or happy or need help, not just when you want my phenomenal tongue."

His logic was flawed. Sex wasn't easy—not when it came to him. I wanted him with a desperate hunger, but there was more at stake than multiple orgasms. The day with Kayleigh still weighed on me, and my agreement with my dad definitely didn't include another bad boy athlete he'd hate on sight.

Then again, the fastest way to discourage Gavin was to prove him wrong once and for all.

"You're on. We'll come to the game tonight, and you'll get three periods to make me blush while you're playing your ass off." I stepped closer to him, and his fingers flexed. "And when I win, I'm going to take great joy in proving you're just like everyone else."

"Game on," he said, and finally made his way up the stairs.

17

Eva

Stephen was my favorite person on the planet. Except when he annoyingly insisted I was wrong.

"You should have told him I wasn't your date," he argued while setting his Louis Vuitton travel bag on the couch.

I shoved my hands in the pocket of my TU hoodie and counted to five. "He didn't care. Gavin oozes confidence, whether it's deserved or not."

Stephen sighed wistfully. "I love a man who knows what he wants."

"Sure, but in this case, he wants me. Not just sex. Me."

"Even better. I was already on Team Gavin, and you're not changing my mind. Did you talk to him about Kayleigh?" He looked at me expectantly, but I shook my head.

"I haven't had the chance."

With a sharp laugh, Stephen flopped on the couch. "I never thought I'd see the day Evangeline Adams was afraid of something."

I kicked his ankle with the toe of my boot. "Don't get comfortable. We have to leave in a couple of minutes."

Stephen stretched his arms along the back of the cushions and tilted his head to stare at me. "You can't distract me by changing the subject. I know you."

The echo of Gavin's words earlier made my voice sharper than normal. "It's not a distraction, and I'm not afraid of asking him."

"Who gave you the information about Kayleigh?"

I crossed my arms and glared at him. "Kayleigh did."

He stood and grabbed his leather jacket from the edge of the couch. "She was drunk, *and* she exonerated Gavin. Who told you he was the one involved?"

I marched to the front door and held it open, knowing Stephen liked to take his time leaving. "A girl who worked at Wildcat. She was more than happy to tell me all about the drama."

"Did you fact check her or were you more than happy to take everything she said at face value?"

The truth was I didn't question a single thing she said. I'd already written Gavin off as an asshole, so I wasn't surprised he'd fuck with Kayleigh. Now, though, it seemed far-fetched. I seemed to remember hearing my informant didn't last long working at Wildcat. Even more interesting, she'd named *Gavin*, not Danny, as the culprit.

Stephen let me stew over his question as we drove to the arena, and I didn't like the direction my thoughts were taking me. Danny was the one who officially worked at Wildcat. Gavin working his brother's shifts might be an open secret, but why would the girl I'd talked to be willing to blow their cover?

A couple of puck bunnies with numbers painted on their faces smiled at Stephen as we walked up to the arena, but he barely acknowledged them. "What's Gavin's jersey number?"

I frowned at him. "Fourteen. Why?"

He nodded at the girls, now glaring at me. "You could show your support for him."

"Not interested. I have to dress out for the football game tomorrow. It's nice coming here as a part of the crowd for once."

"Do you know all their jersey numbers?" he asked softly, shifting his eyes toward another group of girls wearing TU hockey apparel decorated with a variety of numbers.

I didn't. I only knew Gavin's because the last time I'd come to a game, I couldn't stop watching him.

"Hmm, nothing to say?" Stephen teased. "It's okay. I think I know the answer."

"Shut up," I muttered, shoving him with my shoulder.

He didn't budge, but he did clear the path for us to the same seats I'd had before. Stephen was tall and lanky, built like a swimmer, and he knew he looked good. We got several overt stares as we settled next to the TU bench again, but he was focused on the guys warming up on the ice.

Like last time, they skated in circles shooting pucks at the goal. I regularly did complicated acrobatic stunts high in the air, but I was impressed by the ease with which the hockey players moved around the pucks and each other.

I waved and smiled at the guys as they skated past the glass, tucking my head onto Stephen's shoulder. Unlike the last time, Gavin didn't look ready to jump through the glass and murder my date, which may or may not have had to do with the lack of his brother causing problems.

Stephen, knowing his role, pressed a kiss to the side of my head and grinned at my roommates. "What's the latest with Carl? And can I say again how weird it is that you call him by his first name?"

I sniffed. "He hasn't earned a title of respect."

"Is he still giving you bullshit busy work?"

"Yeah, and to add insult to injury, his class is basically him bragging about the things he's done at his company. I wouldn't mind so much if he used the anecdotes as case studies and explained how he made each project a success, but I'm not sure he even knows."

"Yikes."

"The worst part is I've lost a lot of respect for his firm. His other three assistants ended up working there in some capacity, but they all used the experience to find better jobs. I think I understand why now."

Stephen stretched his arm behind me. "I realize I'm talking to a brick wall at this point, but I'm going to keep trying. You should take the job that makes you happy, not the one that pays the most."

"I hear what you're saying, and I will take it under advisement."

Stephen snorted and pointed at himself. "This is my 'the fuck you will' face. You'll do what you always do, which is whatever you want. Damn the torpedoes and anyone who gets in your way."

I held up a finger. "Not true. Gavin is in my way, and despite the many, *many* hours I've spent cursing his name, I haven't figured out how to outmaneuver him."

"Good."

"Excuse me, what?"

He gripped my chin and forcibly turned my face toward the ice where Gavin and his team were stretching in a way that could only be described as sexual. "Look at him. He's beautiful, flexible, and he has magic hands. Your reasons for fighting with him are stupid, and at this point, mostly just foreplay. Give in. I've been waiting years for someone to outmaneuver you."

I shook him off. "I've already given in. Twice."

"And yet you're still cranky."

I stuck my tongue out at him, then ignored him in favor of ogling my roommate. Several minutes went by, then Stephen bumped my shoulder.

"I'm sorry I wasn't here yesterday."

A tiny pang of hurt surprised me. "I didn't expect you to be. You have a life. One that doesn't coincide with pampering me on the one day a year when I lose my shit."

He winced. "Did you lose your shit?"

I pressed my lips together, considering. Stephen would feel guilty if I told him it was the hardest anniversary in years, but he'd be ecstatic if I told him about Gavin. Weirdly, I didn't want to. What passed between Gavin and me felt... sacred. I didn't have secrets from Stephen, but I wanted to hold the moments when I'd felt safe close to me.

"It was the usual." The moment of guilt I felt for glossing over it was completely overshadowed by the seed of comfort planted by Gavin.

I was glad when the game started and I could pretend interest in TU's hockey prowess. Well, mostly pretend. I was pretty interested every time Gavin took the ice. He was smooth and fast, and he seemed to have a sixth sense about where the puck was going to be. I liked athletes—liked watching them do amazing things with their bodies—and Gavin was elite.

He played with a graceful brutality I found beautiful. I'd never admit it, but I'd been watching highlights of their previous games and trying to learn the rules. With the action happening in front of me, I had a hard time remembering the difference between icing and offsides.

Despite the fast-paced game, I was keeping up until right before the first intermission. Gavin flattened a guy against the glass right in front of me. The world slowed down, and his eyes came up to meet mine with a possessive heat. My breath caught in my chest, and goosebumps rose on my skin. Half a second of sexy eye contact, and I was ready to drag Gavin to the nearest dark corner.

I thought he'd take the moment to make his move, but he shifted and took off with the puck. The guy he'd squished chased after him, and at the last second, Gavin passed the puck to Reece, who flicked it in for a goal. The red light behind the net went off to cheers all around us.

The buzzer rang for the end of the period, and all the guys skated off the ice. Stephen nudged me to ask about food, but the best I could tell him was to look near where we came in. I'd assumed all the players had left to do whatever it was they did between periods, but when my gaze skimmed over the empty bench, my eyes locked with Gavin, standing at the entrance to the tunnel behind it.

He'd taken his helmet off, and when our eyes met, he raised a brow. I was almost certain he wasn't supposed to be lingering there, but no one else seemed to notice. His hair was all over the place, his chest rose and fell with quick breaths, and the same tension from earlier coiled inside me. As I watched, he slowly grinned and raised his bare hand to his mouth. His tongue flicked out to lick his fingers, just like he had last night.

Heat raced up my neck into my cheeks and flooded my core. I slapped my hands to my face, but it was too late. He nodded my way, then turned and disappeared into the darkness.

Fuck.

I sank lower into my seat and dropped my head back onto the hard plastic. My face tingled with warmth, along with the rest of me. I was horny, not embarrassed, but it didn't matter. Gavin had made me blush. He'd won the damn bet.

18

Gavin

The house was empty. I didn't know how I knew, but when Eva was home, there was a charge in the air. A subtle feeling of excitement. I hadn't seen her car on the street, but sometimes she had to park farther down. Our driveway/garage situation wasn't meant for four cars.

After morning skate, we usually came home for a few hours to relax before our second game of the week. Today, I didn't feel very relaxed. I was all coiled up with anticipation of battling with my roommate about our bet, which I'd won.

Honestly, I wasn't surprised she'd dipped—she hated losing—but after tossing my backpack on the couch, I noticed a distinct lack of bird noises as well.

"Where's Henry?" I looked at Cole, who shrugged.

Mase had already disappeared downstairs, and Reece was shoulders deep in the fridge. Usually, Henry waited for us in the living room, probably because Reece gave her treats every time we came home.

"Here you go, baby girl," he crooned, right on cue with a handful of strawberries.

Henry loved strawberries, and Reece kept some on hand for her. When he turned away from the fridge though, our house duck was nowhere to be seen. Reece made a clicking noise with his tongue, and Cole rolled his eyes.

"She's not a squirrel. Eva probably brought her along."

It hadn't occurred to me Eva wouldn't be home when we got here. Her presence might have been the reason I'd rushed the guys out of the locker room. Last night, she'd left with the rich-looking guy as soon as the game ended.

And she hadn't come home. At least, not right away. She'd texted me to admit defeat, and to tell me not to worry, she was in good hands. I admit I reacted poorly to the idea she'd voluntarily gone out with her date. Instead of rehashing the game like we usually did, I'd holed up in my room to finish the response paper I'd abandoned on Thursday to chase her to the Kappa party.

Eva was exactly the type to enact revenge by disappearing. I'd pissed her off by spending the night at Jaden and Killsy's apartment, and now she was showing me what it felt like to be on the other end. I appeased my temper by reminding myself she wouldn't react if she didn't care. At some point, we'd need to air out all our issues because this shit wasn't healthy.

After a second, Cole's words registered in my mind, and I caught his arm as he passed me heading for the stairs. "Brought her along where?"

Cole sent me a look that clearly said I was stupid. "The football game? TU plays at noon today, and she's a cheerleader. Where do you think she goes most Saturdays?"

I checked my watch and cursed. The game had already started, so I wouldn't be talking to her until tonight after my game at the earliest.

Reece grunted and spoke with a mouth full of strawberries. "You could go too. It's not like she isn't used to you following her around like a lovesick puppy."

Cole pointed at him. "That's a great idea, actually. She's come to our games a couple of times now. We should go support her. She'd love it."

I was almost sure she wouldn't love it. She'd been a part of the football crew for years, and since this semester started, she'd been mostly hanging with us at the house during her down time. I didn't have a problem with football players, despite what I'd said to Eva the night she moved in, but she seemed to be setting a very firm boundary between our group and theirs.

The memory of Eva patiently explaining stunts to us in the living room gave me another idea. "I think she'd love it more if we went to one of her cheer competitions."

Both guys turned to stare at me.

Cole spoke up first. "I love this idea for us. We should surprise her. I don't think any of her other friends come to those competitions."

Reece pushed up the sleeves of his shirt and turned on the water in the sink. "An auditorium of cheerleaders who haven't had the pleasure of meeting me? I'm in."

He grabbed the dish soap and started washing the pile we'd left on the counter after breakfast. We took turns doing the dishes when Eva wasn't here because we weren't total dicks. She was busy all the time with cheering for the TU teams, working on her own competition skills, and her classes. I was surprised she was able to work in the dates her dad was pushing on her.

A little stab of guilt pricked me as I realized I wasn't much better about demanding her time. Something else we should probably discuss.

Cole grabbed a banana and started up the stairs. "Since

we're not going to the football game and my girl Henry isn't here, I'm taking a nap. Wake me up when it's time to head back."

Reece snorted. "Wake yourself up."

I shook my head and grabbed my wallet and keys from my backpack. The football team was doing well this season, and I had some friends on the team. It wouldn't be a hardship to watch them play while Eva cheered. Normally, I'd be heading for a nap too, but the guilt hadn't dissipated. She'd come to my game last night. I could go to hers today.

Reece gave me the side eye when I opened the door, but he didn't say anything. I still heard him loud and clear. *Chasing after her like a lovesick puppy.* He wouldn't understand—his idea of a serious relationship was hooking up with the same girl twice.

I patently refused to analyze my actions as I drove to the stadium. Cole wanted to nap—I wanted to watch some live football. And see my hot as sin roommate in a cheerleading uniform.

Our football games regularly sold out, but I knew a lot of the stadium staff because they often worked the ice arena too. Parking was a bitch like usual, but my friend, Dougie, was working the west gate.

"Hey man," I bumped his fist. "Can I get a pass?"

"Sure thing. You played like a beast last night." He unlocked the door and pulled it aside enough for me to slip through.

"Thanks, Dougie. Let me know next time your wife isn't on rotation for a home game. I'll get you tickets."

"Hell yeah. I'll hit you up."

I paused just inside the dim hallway and turned back. "Hey Dougie, where are the cheerleaders hanging out today?"

He gave me a big grin. "I got you, fam. Section D, all the way at the front."

"Thanks, brother."

Dougie waved and secured the door behind me. I shoved my hands in my pockets and made my way to section D, where I had to squeeze past a group of teenage girls wearing #playRJ shirts.

The tunnel emptied out into open air seating about fifteen rows back from the field near the TU endzone. Even from my position, I could spot Eva and the other cheerleaders on the sidelines facing the crowd. Her short red and black skirt molded to her hips, and the top was little more than a sports bra with white stripes crisscrossing the TU logo. She had a big black and red bow in her pink-streaked hair, and I suddenly understood Reece's obsession with cheerleaders.

Eva gave the crowd a wide smile and a wave, then backflipped into the waiting hands of her stunt partner, who tossed her into the air with ease. She spun several times before coming to a stop with her arms in a V above her. I'd seen this move at their practice. She wasn't looking my direction, but I eased a little farther into the shadows anyway.

From the row to my right, I heard a deep voice shout her full name. "Evangeline, kill it, sweet cheeks!"

I tore my gaze away from Eva to scan the audience, and my brows shot up when I spotted the guy from last night wearing Henry in a baby carrier across his chest. Well, fuck. I didn't expect him to still be around. Even worse, Eva had trusted him with Henry, and the guy didn't seem at all bothered to be wearing a duck.

Henry, for her part, looked like she was chittering happily at the girl sitting next to them wearing a Mackenzie jersey. The guy smiled and waved, drawing my attention back to Eva, who blew him a kiss.

Fury hit me, fast and hard. She didn't date? There was sure as hell something more than her dad's meddling happening here. Jealousy crept under the anger. Eva smiled at him with her whole heart. The real Eva, who'd only shown up in glimpses when she thought no one was watching.

The same feeling washed over me as when I snuck into her cheer practice. What was I doing here? Fighting for a girl who wanted to hate me?

I knew—I *knew*—Eva wanted more in her life than what she allowed herself. Maybe all our animosity was because we recognized what was inside the other person. The pain, the emptiness, the loss. She gave herself completely to the people she loved, but she refused to let them do the same for her.

My gaze stayed trained on her as she clapped and waved, cheering for her friends on the field. If the guy in the stands made her happy, I wasn't going to get in the way, no matter how much I wanted to be the one. Pain zipped through my chest at the thought of backing off, and I rubbed the phantom ache.

I should never have offered that deal. At the very least, I should have let her pay her way instead of coming up with arbitrary rules and stipulations to keep her close to me.

My thoughts were so loud, I didn't notice Eva's date make his way to the tunnel until he'd almost reached me. I would have turned and left immediately if he didn't give me a nod.

"Hey man, you're Gavin, right? Eva's roommate? I'm Stephen, her back home bestie. Nice to finally meet you." He held out his hand, and I shook it.

Relief flashed through me. Not a date. I had to laugh at Eva's maneuvering. No way in hell was I backing off now. She was going to pay for letting me think I was competing with her friend, and I was going to enjoy every second of it.

His eyes gleamed with amusement as if he could read my mind. "Sorry for stealing her away last night. Great game, by the way. That goal in the first period was hot." He fanned himself, and Henry quacked in outrage at the sudden movement. "I wanted to ask… is the center on your line into dudes by any chance?"

The last vestige of my jealousy disappeared as I seriously considered his question. Reece was definitely into girls, but I genuinely didn't know if he was *only* into girls. His life philosophy was he'd try anything once, so I wasn't about to cock block him if he might be interested.

"You'll have to ask him, but he's not looking for a relationship."

Stephen's eyes cut to Eva. "Sounds like someone else I know, but we're going to change her mind, aren't we?"

A smile crept over my lips at the vote of confidence. "Yes, we are."

Eva's partner threw her into the air again, and she spun around several times until she stopped abruptly facing the crowd. The sheer strength impressed the hell out of me, but Eva's skill made the stunts look easy.

"How does she not get dizzy with all that spinning?" I mused.

"She spots. Keeps her eyes on one steady point to orient her. She's good at that." He raised his brows at me in a clear message.

I cast a speculative look at my sneaky roommate. "I'm messing with her balance, but she doesn't know I'll catch her. Every time."

Stephen clapped me on the back, earning another quack from Henry. "I knew I'd like you. Let's get a drink and talk about the date you're taking her on. My suggestion? Ice skating..."

19

Gavin

A few days later, I took great pleasure in bursting through Eva's door early in the morning on the one day she normally slept in. "Wakey, wakey, Princess."

She shot up in bed with a gasp, her hair wild around her face. "Is Henry okay?"

"She's fine. Having breakfast with Cole. I'm calling in the date you owe me." I crossed my arms and leaned against her doorframe, already dressed and ready for the outing I'd planned.

Eva shoved her hair back and glared at me. "Unless you have coffee on you, get out."

I grinned and pulled the chilled glass bottle from my back pocket. "This coffee?"

With a growl, she crawled off the bed to snatch it out of my hand. Feral Eva might be my favorite version of her. Well, second favorite after the version where she's naked and wild underneath me.

She popped the lid and took a long drink, then met my

eyes with slightly less murder in her expression. "You want to go on a date *now*?"

"Yes. You have this morning off, and the rink is free."

Her brows drew together. "The rink?"

"We're going ice skating."

Eva blinked like she hadn't heard me right, and her lips parted in a silent question.

I couldn't resist dropping a quick kiss on her surprised mouth. "Get ready. I have a breakfast sandwich and another coffee waiting for you downstairs."

A pretty pink flush started at the top of the shirt she slept in and crawled up her neck. "What if I say no?"

I booped her nose. "Can't. You lost the bet fair and square, Princess. If you can't skate, I'm happy to teach you, but we're spending the morning on the ice."

Her lips pressed together, and her chin lifted. "Fine, but I'm not dressing up for you."

"Just wear something you can move in," I told her as she closed the door in my face.

Stephen had warned me the key to getting her to agree was to spring it on her at the last second. She excelled at finding loopholes, so I needed to minimize the time for her to react.

I'd give her ten minutes, then come back up.

She was ready in eight, and I should have realized then I'd already lost. The living room was empty when she came downstairs in sleek gray leggings and a cropped white sweater. Every time she moved, I got a flash of her tight abs and tanned skin.

"Let's get this over with," she grumbled.

I handed her the napkin wrapped breakfast sandwich and the second coffee. "Don't get too excited. I'm not sure I can handle your enthusiasm."

"You know," she started in an innocent tone. "You could handle me just fine if we were upstairs and naked."

I chuckled. "Watch it, Princess. You almost sounded like you were willing to risk a messy relationship."

She scoffed. "Who said anything about a relationship? I recently decided I was willing to risk a messy couple of hours in bed."

I reached for her free hand and dropped a kiss on her wrist before leading her out the door. "When I finally get you naked in a bed, it's going to be days, not hours."

Eva tilted her head in my direction, awarding me the point in our battle of wills. I ushered her into my car, and she stared out the window, methodically eating her breakfast over the short drive to the arena.

She excused herself to use the bathroom once we got inside, and I had a few minutes to stand at the edge of the rink and breathe. I loved the ice. The quiet stillness of a fresh rink touched something inside me, allowed me to let go of all the shit holding me back and fly. At least, it used to. Before every move I made was weighed and judged.

When Stephen suggested I take Eva ice skating for our date, I'd thought he might be kidding—until he laid it out for me. Eva couldn't be seen dating anyone not approved by her father or she'd lose her funding, so we needed to go somewhere private. Somewhere she could relax and have fun. Somewhere I had an excuse to touch her at will.

I got my wish. The rink hadn't opened to the public yet, but the Zamboni had already flooded the ice. Most of the lights were off, leaving the stands dark and only the ice lit. I already had a space set up with my bag, my skates, and a pair I'd borrowed from the equipment room for her.

When she emerged from the women's locker room, her gaze locked onto me, and I saw the way her lips tipped up.

Eva had complained about the early hour, but anticipation lit her eyes. And she couldn't look away any more than I could.

"This is the strangest date," she grumbled, taking a seat next to me on the bench.

I laughed. "Have you ever *been* on a date?"

She lifted her nose with an affronted air and shoved her foot into her first skate. "I've been on dates, ass. They usually involve food and some form of entertainment, preferably the naked kind."

Her gaze dragged over my sweats, and I resisted the urge to start stripping immediately. She was trying to use sex to distance us, exactly as Stephen predicted. I wasn't taking the easy out.

"This should be plenty entertaining, and I provided food *and* coffee this morning."

Eva's eyes narrowed. "True, but you also barged in on my sleeping time. I'll give you a pass since you provided the right kind of coffee."

"Are you going to stall all morning or are we going to skate?"

She blew a strand of hair away from her face. "I'm going as fast as I can. Not all of us are hockey superstars."

"Here let me." I crouched in front of her and reached for the second skate she was struggling with. Eva didn't protest as I tightened and tied the laces. I let my hand drift up her calf as I released her, and she rewarded me with a tiny inhale.

I stood and took her hand, intending to help her get to the ice, but when she rose with fluid grace, only inches separated us.

"Since you like bets so much, how about another one?"

Intrigued, I ran my thumb over her fingers. "What are we betting on?"

Eva glanced over my shoulder at the rink. "A race. Double or nothing. If I win, *you* hire a cleaning service."

"What about the grocery shopping and food prep?"

She shrugged one shoulder. "I'd be getting food delivered anyway. It's not too much harder to add you guys to the order."

"And if I win?"

Her icy eyes blazed with fire, and she shifted forward until I felt her breath on my lips. "You get another date."

"You're on," I whispered, sealing it with a surprisingly sweet kiss.

Eva leaned into me, silently asking for more, but I wasn't rushing this. I eased away, brushing my nose along hers. If this date didn't show her how good it could be between us, I'd try another. And another. Until every one of her walls had crumbled at my feet.

I could be very stubborn when it came to something—or someone—I wanted.

Her bet simply gave me an easy in. Clearly, I'd prefer if she admitted she wanted another date rather than using a thinly veiled excuse, but at this point, I'd take what I could get. She wasn't going to win a race with me. Case in point, she nearly fell over as soon as we moved toward the open door.

I steadied her with my hands at her hips. "Do you want me to give you some pointers first?"

She slapped at my touch. "How hard could it be? You just glide around in circles."

I chuckled. "Okay, Princess. You sure you want to do this?"

Her jaw firmed, and she gripped the sideboards as she

carefully eased herself out onto the ice. "Yes. We race from here to the far blue line. I'll count down from three, and we go on 'go'."

With a shake of my head, I lined up next to her. "Whenever you're ready."

"Three, two, one... go!"

I pushed off lazily, ready to catch her if she fell, but Eva was already gone. She took off in a blaze of speed, and by the time I realized I needed to catch her, the race was over.

Eva crossed the line seconds ahead of me and flipped herself around to skate backward at a fast clip with a huge grin on her face. "What's the matter, Gavin? Not used to losing on the ice?"

I let out a laugh. Stephen had played me—Eva had played me—but I still had what I'd wanted. Time with her in a place where she didn't have to be anyone but herself. I caught up to her easily and matched her speed, biding my time. She was smiling at me, full of joy, and I'd gladly lose a million races to keep that look on her face.

"Clever. I especially liked the wobble when you stood up."

Eva gave a little bow. "You think I spent my youth as a pampered princess and didn't go through an ice-skating phase?"

"I concede defeat."

"Yesss," she hissed, executing a quick spin. "No more bacon pans for me."

"You know what this means?" I asked while slowly closing the distance between us.

The tone in my voice must have warned her because Eva stopped her victory dance and sent me a wary look. "What?"

"I have no reason to hold back now." I sprinted toward

her, and she didn't have time to move before I caught her hips and hauled her over my shoulder.

Eva squealed and gripped my underlayer in two tight fists, curling herself as close to me as she could get. "Put me down, you psycho."

I slid my hand up her thigh, slowing down as I circled the rink. "No, I think I like you where you are. Might as well relax and enjoy the ride."

My thumb slipped between her legs, and her breath hit my lower back with puff of warm air. "Gavin."

She didn't say anything else, but I recognized the yearning in her voice. Eva was so responsive to me, a simple touch was enough to have her wet and waiting. According to Stephen, she was always disappointed because she only picked hookups she could control—but she couldn't control this. Our bet at the game was a prime example.

I flexed my fingers and slowed my speed, so I could lean forward. "Let go. I'll catch you."

Eva understood what I wanted her to do and released her grip. I shifted her weight from my shoulder to my arms, setting her skates back on the ice. She caught herself with a hand behind my neck, and I drew us both upright again. My arms stayed locked around her, and her lips curved up at the edges.

"Had any experience couples skating?" she asked.

"A little." With a tiny push, I set us in motion with her tucked neatly between my skates.

20

Gavin

I was as at home on my skates as I was on solid ground, so Eva only had to hold on. We made a slow circle around the rink, and I was reminded of our first morning living together when I'd woken up with her curled around me in my bed.

"Did you know you're a cuddler?" The question slipped out without much thought, but Eva stiffened a little.

"No, I'm not."

I let out a quiet laugh. "Yes, you are. You burrowed right past that pillow wall you erected the first night."

Her fingers tickled the hair at the back of my neck, and she looked away for a long second before raising a brow at me. "How do I know you didn't pull me past the pillow wall? You were the one making sexy eyes."

"How do you know what my eyes looked like? You were facing away from me, trying so hard to prove being in bed with me didn't affect you."

She scoffed. "It didn't."

"So hard," I reiterated.

Eva snickered. "I wasn't the one who was hard."

"That's not going to change any time soon, Princess."

She let out a little huff, then chewed on her lower lip, like she was debating her next thought.

"Go ahead," I encouraged her.

"Cole mentioned you were supposed to go to another school up north. How did you end up at TU?"

I shifted my grip to stroke the exposed skin of her belly, trying not to shut down at her question. If she'd asked me the night in my bed, I wouldn't have even considered sharing the truth, but Eva wasn't asking so she could use the information against me. She was curious.

"Danny and I both played in the USHL our senior year of high school. Things were going really well, I'd been drafted by Dallas, and had plans to attend University of Ohio, then our parents died."

Eva leaned into me, resting her head on my chest, as we slowly circled the rink.

"Danny didn't take it well. He spiraled, making one bad decision after another while I was trying to deal with lawyers and estate shit. Our team made the championship, and before the game, he came running up to me, begging me for help. Apparently, he'd been fucking around with this girl, and she was threatening to cause problems at the game. Danny's never been good with the aftermath of hookups. I'd been randomly selected for a drug test, but he offered to pee in a cup for me if I got this girl off his back."

When I paused, she lifted her head, her brow furrowed. "He failed the drug test?"

I nodded. "I could have told them the truth, but I still would have been in deep shit for cheating the test. Danny didn't know until our coach announced I'd been disqualified from the game. Ohio found out and revoked my scholarship. Luckily, Dallas still wanted me, and the coach there had an in at TU. Danny came with me to Texas."

"Why would he volunteer knowing he was going to fail?"

"He didn't know he was going to fail. The drugs were supposed to be out of his system, or so he thought. It's never been the same between us. I lost my parents, but I feel like I lost my brother too. I miss him. Most of the time. I like TU though, even if Danny resents me for moving across the country."

"I'm glad you're here," she said quietly.

We circled the rink again, and the warmth in my chest grew. The events around the championship game had changed the course of my life. I hadn't admitted to anyone else—not even myself—how much I regretted the split in my relationship with Danny. We'd both fucked up, but we were here.

With Eva's breath soft against my neck, I couldn't find it in me to regret anything else.

Eva, though, had reached her limit. "I need a drink," she announced before veering off to the door.

Stephen had warned me breaking down her walls wouldn't be easy, and I'd gotten farther than I'd expected before she pulled back. He'd also said not to let her retreat too far. I followed her and dug through my bag while she frowned down the tunnel.

"Here." I handed her a full water bottle and watched her take a long swig. "I met your friend, Stephen, at the football game."

Her brows rose. "That must have been interesting. He didn't tell me you were there."

"He told me to ask about Kayleigh." The request still felt strange because I had no context for it, but the way Eva's eyes narrowed told me Stephen was probably going to regret interfering.

"Do you remember a drunk cheerleader coming into Wildcat a couple of years ago?"

I didn't have to search my memory too hard to bring up an image of a short brunette in a cheer uniform. "Yes..." I wasn't sure where she was going with this, but I had a feeling I wasn't going to like the direction.

"Why did you send her away then call the cops on her?"

I frowned. "I didn't send her away. Wildcat policy said we couldn't serve visibly drunk patrons. When I refused to give her coffee, she got belligerent and stormed out."

"And the cops?"

I ran a hand through my hair, remembering the punch of panic when I'd realized she was getting into a car. "She couldn't even walk straight. I didn't consider she might have driven there until she'd already pulled out into traffic. So I called the police."

Eva's lips pressed together, and she looked away. "Her name is Kayleigh, and she was on my squad. They arrested her. She lost her scholarship and her spot on the team."

The reality of her dislike suddenly became very clear. "You thought I sent her into a trap? I know your first instinct is to protect the people around you, but that girl could have killed someone."

Eva stared down at her hands wrapped around the water bottle. "I believed you could have kept her there and called one of her friends or her coach to come get her."

I shook my head, stunned. "*That's* why you've hated me for the last two years?"

"It seemed like a good reason at the time. Kayleigh asked me to let it go, so I spent the next two years avoiding you and trying not to think about how the callous actions of one person could ruin the future of another." She held up her hand when I went to speak. "I know how that sounds. I hear it."

We sat in silence, with the echo of the empty arena around us, and something shifted. The edge of sharp distance Eva carried around her like armor softened.

She looked up at me, her blue eyes sincere. "I'm sorry. I've been struggling to reconcile this version of you with the one I thought I understood. After you told me about your parents, and Stephen assaulted me with logic, I can see how I was wrong. But it doesn't change anything between us."

I tipped her chin up. "Do you trust me?"

"Yes." She didn't hesitate, and she didn't look away.

"Then give me a chance."

Eva pulled her chin free. "I can admit you're not the evil asshole I thought you were, but there's no future here."

Disappointment hit me square in the chest, but I'd expected her to balk. "Agree to disagree. Come on, you've had enough water. Let's have some fun." I tugged her up from the bench and grabbed the Bluetooth speaker from my bag. "You can tell me about how your cheer competitions are going this year while I stare at your ass."

She laughed, and the fragile tension broke. "I knew you couldn't resist."

"What about you? Come to my games this week and stare at my ass?"

Eva skated out ahead of me as I set up a random playlist, sending me a mischievous smile over her shoulder. "I do like watching you get all sweaty. Can you get me tickets?"

I'd buy a season's worth of tickets if it meant I could look over and see her cheering by the glass. "I think I can figure something out."

> Carter: That's what I'm talking about.

Me: You need a hobby.

I'D LOVE to say we crushed Ridgegate University, but our Friday game came down to a lucky score in the final seconds. Reece passed to me, and I should have sent the puck to Cole for a better shot, but I saw an opening. If I'd missed, we'd have gone into overtime on a tie, but the puck sailed cleanly past their goalie's shoulder.

We had a rematch tomorrow, but tonight, we were celebrating in the locker room.

"Party at our house," Reece shouted over the chaos.

Several of our teammates looked my way for confirmation, and I caved. We had a fire pit in the backyard we barely used, and our new cleaning service was starting tomorrow. They deserved to let loose, but morning skate would suck if half the team was hungover.

"Fine." The cheers were deafening, but I raised my arms to get them to shut up. "No hard liquor, players and plus ones only. This isn't a Kappa party."

I sped through my postgame routine, partly because I wanted to get home before the team, but also because Eva had come to the game. She'd jumped out of her seat when I scored that final goal, and all I wanted to do was find a quiet place to celebrate with her.

Knowing she liked watching me play, I'd shown off a little and taken more chances than normal. Before tonight, I wasn't even sure I'd be able to play the way Dallas wanted—the way I'd been before my life had imploded. Coach had given me a speculative look, but at least Carter seemed happy with it.

Despite my hopes for a speedy exit, Coach wanted to talk to me before I left. I sent Reece, Cole, and Mase home in my car since Sellers volunteered to wait and give me a ride. A heavy sense of apprehension coiled in my stomach as I approached his office.

"You wanted to see me, Coach?"

He looked up from his desk with a smile, which went a long way toward getting rid of the nerves. "I don't know what got into you tonight, but I'm glad you finally found the Gavin King I recruited three years ago."

"Thanks?"

Coach laughed. "Feels good to beat Ridgegate. Make sure you're rested for tomorrow."

He sent a knowing look past me in the doorway to Sellers chasing Jaden around the locker room with what could only be a dirty sock. Jaden tripped over his own shorts, then howled as Sellers slapped him across the face with his improvised weapon.

"I wish I could take no responsibility for these idiots, but they're coming to my house."

Coach waved me off. "Better get moving then. Morning skate waits for no man."

I gathered the rest of my gear and herded the guys outside. Sellers did me a solid and didn't stop for milkshakes as he threatened. My street was crowded with cars, but I didn't see any half-naked people on my lawn. Inside, about a dozen teammates crowded around the living room furniture, at least half of them with girls hanging on them.

"Where's Eva?" I asked Reece.

He shrugged without pulling his attention away from the leggy redhead in his lap. No help there. Cole sauntered up carrying two beers and offered me one. I shook my head and scanned the crowd again.

Cole took a long swallow and nodded at the stairs. "Henry's in my room, if you're worried."

I rolled my eyes. "I'm not worried about the duck. I was looking for Eva."

"Oh, she's in *her* room."

After one more check of the living room to make sure no one was breaking our shit, I decided the guys could handle the rest of the party. I'd waited long enough.

"Make sure this gets cleaned up." My mind was already upstairs, but Cole's next words stopped me in my tracks.

"She's not alone." When I turned on him, he held up his hands. "I wasn't involved. Danny's up there with her."

I remembered Danny's grin at the exhibition game and my stupid insistence from the first week. *I have no interest in Eva. If you like having your balls handed to you, feel free to try.*

Fuck, no. I was *not* letting my asshole brother disappear into Eva's room with her. I took the stairs two at a time.

21

Eva

I hadn't planned on hosting a lowkey hockey party, but I accepted it as a repercussion of living with a bunch of them. Henry was safely sleeping in Cole's room from before the game, and I was holed up in mine putting away clothes, trying to come to terms with my feelings for a certain hockey player who'd looked right at me and tapped his chest after he made the game winning shot.

The ass.

When he'd asked me if I trusted him the other day at the rink, I'd responded without thinking. I hadn't expected to, but I *did* trust him. He knew parts of me even Stephen didn't get to see, and I was struggling. Not with feeling exposed—I knew he'd keep those parts safe—but with the urge to give him everything.

He'd brought up the night we slept together in his bed, and the part I remembered the most was his question when I'd tried to knock him down.

You going to give me access, Princess?

I'd thought he was needling me, trying to get a response because nothing else had worked, but I'd fallen for it anyway. Whether I liked it or not, he had access. What was I going to do about it?

A knock came on my door before I could pin down a response. My heart kicked into high gear, but it wouldn't be Gavin. He didn't knock.

"Yes?"

The door eased open, and for a split second, excitement stole my breath as a dark head peeked through. Then Danny grinned at me, and the anticipation crashed.

"Can I come in?"

My pulse slowed as I tossed the last stack of yoga pants into my dresser. "Why are you up here?"

Danny entered the room, closing the door behind him. "I'll take that as a yes. I'm up here because Gavin is going to be downstairs celebrating his win soon, and I want to ruin his night a little bit."

I raised a brow. "Not much of a brother."

He shrugged one shoulder. "I never claimed to be much of a brother. We all have our issues. Gavin is mine."

The protective part of me roared to life, but I sat neatly on my bed and gestured at my desk chair. "Have a seat. We're talking about this."

When he moved toward the bed, I held up a hand. "Nope. I accept your misguided attempt to irritate Gavin, but I'm not going to be the reason."

"Fair enough." He sat in the chair and swiveled back and forth.

"Why are you such a shit to him?"

Danny laughed quietly. "I thought we were on the same team, Shortcake. Gavin gets everything he wants, everyone else be damned."

I frowned. "You don't believe that, do you?"

He crossed his arms and leaned back, his smile fading.

"Why wouldn't I? He got the college he wanted, the hockey team aimed for the championship, the house, the friends... you."

There was a lot to unpack in his list, but two things stood out. "The house?"

"This is his house. He sold the one our parents left us and used his half to buy this one."

No wonder he hadn't been worried about the landlord. Did the others know? Did it change anything between us? My mind jumped from one question to another while Danny watched me with a little too much pleasure in his gaze.

The asshole was messing with me again, and by extension, Gavin. I didn't doubt he'd told me the truth—it made sense and fit Gavin's personality perfectly—but his motivation was definitely rooted in causing trouble. The house wasn't a big deal. I could talk to Gavin about it later and dish out my own retribution.

I didn't like being played, and I knew how to hit back. He was either truly an asshole, in which case I knew how to deal with him, or he felt guilty for the way things went down with Gavin at their championship.

"Did you tank Gavin's drug test on purpose?"

Danny stiffened and his smile fell away. "He told you?"

"I know a lot of things, Danny. Did you?" I pressed.

He leaned forward, resting his arms on his thighs. "No. I was lazy and sent Gavin out to deal with my mess because I was tired and hungover. It never occurred to me I'd fail the test, no matter what he told you."

His jaw ticked as he stared at me, waiting for an argument or recrimination. If his body language could be trusted, Danny wasn't any happier about the results than Gavin.

"That *is* what he told me, but I like to find things out for myself. Are you sorry?"

He scoffed. "What do you think? I destroyed my brother's future because I couldn't deal with a clingy girl on my own. I'm pissed at him most of the time for just *handling* everything so easily, but I never wanted to hurt him."

"Then why do you keep making his life hard?"

Danny pushed away from the chair to pace back and forth. "Because it's not hard, and he doesn't get it. Everything he touches turns to gold, and I can't even figure out what I want to do with my life. He doesn't have to agree every time I ask him to do something for me. I could probably have taken that econ test myself, but why not use Gavin's golden touch to get ahead for once?"

My instincts perked up at his last sentence. "It's convenient for you that he's able to do well in your classes."

He snorted. "Yeah, except for the lit test last year, but how was I supposed to know the prof was going to change the assignment at the last minute to a book Gavin hadn't read."

So that was Gavin's big secret. The drug test scandal had already played out, and he'd done a fabulous job of keeping attention off himself for the last three years—because he'd been helping his brother cheat his way through college.

If I wanted to hurt Gavin, I had more than enough information to ruin his future the way he'd ruined Kayleigh's.

The thing was... I didn't. Hurting Gavin had lost its appeal about the time he offered me a duck-friendly place to live. Over the last few months, I'd learned he'd do anything to help the people he loved—and sometimes the ones he tolerated. Gavin had tried to protect Kayleigh and all the other people on the road that day.

He tried to protect his teammates from me, he protected

me from my questionable dates, and he protected Danny the only way Danny would allow. By helping him stay afloat when he needed time to figure himself out.

I wished Danny would get his head out of his ass and stop making things harder on Gavin. If he'd let Gavin in instead of pushing him away, they could both be happy. A tingling sensation started in my chest and moved outward as I put my last thought into a different context.

It wasn't the same with us. It *wasn't*.

Danny stopped pacing to fiddle with the junk on my dresser, and I braced myself to ask about the other thing on his list I hadn't expected.

He beat me to it. "I've never seen him this lost on a girl, by the way. Random hookups, yeah, but hockey has always been his only priority."

Danny was wrong. Gavin had other priorities besides hockey, namely his brother. I highly doubted I was on that short list.

He turned and held up the tickets delivered to me yesterday, two VIP entries to my dad's first political fundraiser. "When are you going to tell him he's competing for the hand of a future senator's daughter?"

I hopped up and snatched them away, putting them back on the dresser facedown. "It's not important because I don't date."

"Could have fooled me. Seems like every time I see you there's another guy hanging all over you. What… does Gavin not meet daddy's standards?"

My stomach twisted at the thought of my dad learning about Gavin. I'd forgotten Danny knew about the dating agreement thanks to eavesdropping on my conversation with Stephen. A rookie mistake.

"Oh, so now you *want* him to get what he wants?"

Danny grinned. "I'm not a monster. You're good for him. He's been playing better since you started your little game, and if the way he looks at you is any indication, he's only biding his time before he makes his move."

"What makes you think he hasn't made it and been shot down?"

He spread his arms, encompassing my room. "He's not in here right now. I like you, Shortcake, but I hope he wins this one."

A flutter in my chest warned me he wasn't the only one. I liked Gavin. A lot. More than I was supposed to. Danny was right though. Gavin didn't meet my dad's standards, and I'd signed away my right to choose my dates until I graduated.

Even if I gave in, we'd have to hide the relationship, and Gavin deserved better than a half-assed girlfriend. Goosebumps rose on my skin at the term I'd never associated with myself, but the heavy kernel of fear never appeared. The deep-down feeling of never being good enough had faded to a faint shiver.

With Gavin, I always felt worthy.

As if he knew I'd been weakening toward him, my door burst open. No question who it was this time. Gavin strode inside, hair still wet from his shower at the arena, sweats riding low on his hips, and I had to lock my knees to keep from taking a step toward him.

Gavin's gaze swept the room, pausing to check me over before shifting to glare at his brother. The two men faced each other, so similar at first glance, but I had no problem seeing Gavin's ingrained confidence next to Danny's thinly veiled resentment.

"Get out," Gavin growled at his brother.

Danny hesitated a second, and I knew with every fiber in my body if he didn't start moving, Gavin would physically remove him. Quickly and possibly painfully. Danny must have read the intentions on Gavin's face because for once he didn't say anything snide back, just left. I didn't spare him a glance when he closed the door softly behind him.

I cocked my head at the man who refused to let me dismiss him. "Can I help you with something, Gavin?"

He stalked forward, and I didn't move an inch. The frustration and anger on his face when he'd barreled inside was replaced with a possessive heat making me wetter than I'd ever experienced. What the hell was wrong with me?

I lifted a brow, maintaining eye contact as he approached. "Well? You're prowling around, ordering people out of *my* space. You must need something, right?"

"You. I need you."

My heart flipped over at his rough words. I should have realized the second I let Danny into my room. I was already lost.

"I have a proposition." He wasn't going to like it, but it was all I could offer at the moment.

Gavin stopped in front of me, his chest rising and falling in uneven breaths. "What more do you want from me, Princess?"

"You can have me, but no one can know."

He shook his head slowly. "I want more than sex."

I swallowed and said the words I'd sworn weren't for me. "Me too. I'll give you a chance, with all the benefits and consequences until one of us says otherwise, but we can't make it public. No one can know."

"You don't know what you're asking for."

I laughed, a little bit hurt he hadn't jumped on my offer. "I'm acutely aware of what I'm asking for. I'm just not convinced you can give it to me."

"And you think Danny can?" He sounded like he was on

the verge of chasing Danny downstairs and making himself an only child. Maybe I was more like Danny than I wanted to admit, but I couldn't resist pushing Gavin to take my deal.

"What's the matter, Gavin?" I taunted. "Not willing to share with your little brother?"

He wrapped his hand around my throat, not squeezing, only holding me in place. "Let's get one thing clear. I will *never* share you. For however long we're doing this, you're mine. Understand?"

I nodded, a tiny movement at odds with the overwhelming pressure in my chest.

His thumb traced the column of my neck to lift my chin. "I want to hear the words, Princess."

"I'm yours," I repeated, feeling the last of my resistance fall.

"Right answer," he whispered, putting pressure on my chin to part my lips.

22

Eva

Heat flared in his eyes as he dropped his mouth to mine. His hand slid around my neck to tangle in my hair, and I opened for him without a second thought. Gavin kissed me slowly, thoroughly, savoring me as if he had all the time in the world.

I melted.

I knew what he could do to my body, but his kisses unwound me. He felt like coming home, like I belonged here, with him. I exhaled my surrender, and the hunger snapped taut. Gavin made a low noise of encouragement, and I scrabbled at the hem of his shirt, yanking it up.

"Off," I grunted.

He released me long enough to reach behind him and pull the shirt over his head, leaving him in only black sweats that slid even lower as his abs flexed. I spread my fingers over the chest I'd been dreaming about since the first night, past the tattoos on his ribs, down to the deep V of muscles disappearing into his waistband.

With his hands on my hips, he walked me backward until we hit a wall. Thankfully, I hadn't put any of my art up because this was a much better use for the space. Before I could get my hands on his cock, he lifted my sweater, taking my arms with it, leaving me in only my sheer bra. I shivered at the cool air on my torso, and Gavin captured both my wrists in one hand, holding them above my head.

I wanted him to touch me, but he trailed his knuckles down my body, barely grazing my skin. I thought I might spontaneously combust if he kept teasing me.

"Gavin," I barked out.

He responded with a slow grin. "You're not in charge tonight, Princess. We're taking our time."

I let my head thunk back against the wall and tried to tug my hands free. He leaned into me, putting pressure on my wrists and dropping his head to flick his tongue over my hard nipple. Fire shot straight to my core, making me quiver.

"So impatient," he murmured, switching to the other side while I writhed. "Is this what you want?"

He slid a hand inside my leggings and rubbed a slow circle on my clit. My hips shot off the wall, and I let out a whimper. I couldn't string two words together if I tried—I just needed him to keep touching me.

"So wet for me. Is this what I have waiting for me after my games?"

"Please…" I begged.

He laughed, low and rough. "Okay, baby, since you asked so nicely."

With his thumb on my clit and his mouth against my ear, he fucked me with his fingers.

"I imagine you like this everywhere. In the shower, in class, in bed, after every goal on the ice. It's always you."

I moved my hips to meet him, but he had total control.

The orgasm hit me out of nowhere. I couldn't do anything except hold on.

After I stopped shuddering, Gavin let go of my hands and crouched in front of me to peel off my leggings. My breath sawed in and out of my lungs as I used his broad shoulders to shift my weight from one foot to the other.

"I swear to god if you leave I will murder you in your sleep," I warned him.

Gavin grinned up at me, naked and shaky because of him. "This was only the warmup. You're beautiful when you come, and I intend to enjoy the sight all night long."

I smacked his shoulder. "If we stay up all night, you're going to be dragging ass at your game tomorrow."

Gavin kissed my hip. "Worth it."

His hands tracked up the backs of my legs to my ass, and he lifted me as he stood. I caught myself on his shoulders, locking my ankles behind his waist. The sweats did nothing to contain his cock. His hard length pressed against my sensitive clit, and I couldn't help tipping my hips a little.

Gavin's fingers tightened, and he rocked forward with me. "Condom?"

"I'm on birth control, but I don't have one."

"I do." In seconds, he'd walked us through the bathroom to his room.

One hand gripped my hair, pulling my head back so he could drag his mouth up my throat, then claim me with a possessive kiss. I didn't even notice him lower me to the bed. He reached behind him to squeeze my ankle, and I let him go.

Gavin raised a brow as he backed toward his nightstand and pulled out a box of condoms. "Technically, we have you to thank for these."

"I am so smart," I muttered, making a gimme gesture with my fingers.

He opened the box, plucked one out, and tossed it at me, then kicked off his pants. I froze halfway through tearing into the packet when his erection sprang free. Damn, the man was beautiful everywhere.

And he was all mine.

Gavin knelt on the bed, wedging his shoulders between my legs so he could give me a long, slow lick from slit to clit. I gasped, grasping the bedspread next to me as electric heat zipped up my body.

"I've been dying for another taste of you." He reached up to take the condom from me and gave my clit another flick with his tongue. "But I've been dreaming of burying myself inside you since I woke up that first morning."

"Only since then?" I gasped, threading my fingers through his silky hair and tugging.

His eyes rose to meet mine, shadowed with hunger, and his lips curled up at the edges in the smug smile I used to hate. "No, not only since then."

"Good," I whispered, drawing him up until he was seated between my thighs.

A quick swipe through my wetness, then he notched himself at my entrance. "Are you going to come for me, Princess?"

I hooked my hand behind his neck and pulled him down for a drugging kiss. "Only for you."

He thrust forward, and we both drew in a shuddering breath. My nails dug into his shoulder as the pleasure mixed with a fine edge of pain. His back flexed under my fingers from the effort of holding himself still, but I didn't want stillness. I didn't want slow. I wanted him to fuck me like he meant it.

And he already knew that.

Gavin pulled back slowly, then snapped forward again. And again. Finding a brutal rhythm that made me forget everything except him. He whispered dirty words of praise in my ear, and I curled a leg tight against his side, urging him deeper.

"Fuck, Eva, you feel so good." Gavin knew how to move his hips, knew when to speed up and when to take it slow, knew when I needed a little more finesse. He knew me—and I was pretty damn certain he was going to ruin me for all other men.

I let go, and Gavin brought me the dark pleasure of surrender I'd been missing.

A COUPLE OF HOURS LATER, I woke to silence. The party sounds had died down, but Gavin still held me tight, pressed against my back with his arms locked around me. The weak light of dawn spilled in from the uncovered window, and I had a scattered memory of his hand on my stomach, my head pillowed on his bicep. More of a feeling than a distinct image.

He clearly hadn't been lying about the cuddling, not that I'd really doubted him. I wiggled, intending to roll over, but his arm tightened, holding me in place.

"Stay," he whispered, his voice rough with sleep.

"I'm not going anywhere," I said softly.

"Good." He nuzzled closer, his breath warm on my neck. "I want you here every morning."

Now that I'd reassured him I wasn't a flight risk, he relaxed enough to let me turn to face him. "If I stayed here every night, we'd both drop dead from exhaustion."

His lips brushed my temple as he pulled me closer. "I'm willing to risk it."

"If I'd known you were insatiable, I might have given in earlier."

Gavin chuckled. "If I was insatiable, your mouth would be too busy to talk right now."

The unmistakable length of his erection pressed into my stomach, and a slow burn started in my blood. "Talking is overrated." I kissed his shoulder, his chest, and started drifting downward, but he stopped me with a groan.

"Princess, as much as I want your mouth on my cock, we don't have time." He nodded at the digital clock on his desk. "I have to get ready for morning skate soon."

"Fine," I burrowed closer, curling my bent leg over his hip so his cock lined up squarely with my clit.

He gripped my thigh, his fingers digging into my skin, and a low rumble came from his chest. His hips canted forward as me pulled me closer, and we both groaned.

"You going to be waiting for me here after my game tonight?" Gavin loosened his hold, rolling me under him and scooting lower to suck a nipple into his mouth.

"Unfair," I moaned. "If I can't use my mouth, you can't use yours."

He chuckled against my breasts, snaking his hand between us. "You didn't answer my question."

"Mmm." I was having trouble stringing together words while he stroked me with one finger, then two, rubbing my clit with every slow thrust of his hips.

"Use your words, baby. Where are you going to be?"

"Here," I gasped. "Thought you were leaving."

"You can give me one before I have to go," he whispered. "Let me see you come."

I didn't last long at all. Not with his weight on top of me, his fingers building a steady pressure, and his voice in my ear. I climaxed as pleasure rolled over me in waves.

Gavin kissed me slow and sweet. "That's my girl."

And I was. I was completely his. Somehow, I wasn't freaking out, but the liquid heat in my muscles might have had something to do with it. A tinge of sadness lurked under all the warm, gooey feelings though. When Gavin climbed out of bed to get ready, I figured out the cause.

I didn't want him to leave. I wanted to finish what we'd started, then curl up next to him and fall asleep in his arms again. Jesus. We'd been together for twelve hours and I was already an emotional mess.

While Gavin was dressing, one of the guys pounded on his door to give him a five-minute warning, and I was glad they hadn't simply barged in like they tended to do with me. We needed to keep this relationship a secret if I wanted to finish my last semester of school, but I wasn't sure we could hide it from our roommates.

Sooner or later, they'd figure it out. I trusted them not to make a big deal of it, even Reece, but the more people who knew, the more likely someone would slip up.

Gavin came back to the bed to give me a lingering kiss, ignoring the continued shouting from the hallway. "Get some sleep. I'll see you later."

A dark cloud settled over me after he left, but I pushed the foreboding aside to focus on my immediate future. I had the house to myself, a cleaning crew was coming in a few hours to make it shine, and I'd woken up surrounded by an irresistibly sexy man. If someone else were describing the scenario, I'd declare them a lucky bitch and we'd move on. No over-analysis necessary.

I decided to take Stephen's advice and enjoy the moment.

Today, I was embracing my inner lucky bitch. I napped in his bed until mid-morning, then spent my down time taking care of errands and spoiling Henry. Gavin texted me increasingly dirty messages throughout the day, and when he came home after winning his game, I was naked and waiting in his bed. As promised.

23

Gavin

Eva didn't suddenly start spending every night with me, but it was close. Her assistantship heated up, so she was busy with a bonus project on top of all her other responsibilities. During the day, we barely saw each other, but at night, she was mine.

Danny dropped by once while she was in class to smugly tell me he'd aced the econ test. It was his way of thanking me, and for once, he didn't ask for money. I wasn't sure what to think of the change, but I didn't spare it a lot of thought. Danny went through phases. I had my own shit to deal with.

Namely, I seemed to have garnered Dallas' attention again after three years of succinct brush offs. Carter was ecstatic. I knew I was playing different—better—but it wasn't a conscious decision. Eva came to as many games as she could, mostly on Fridays since football overlapped with our hockey schedule. Every time I looked into the stands and saw her there screaming for me, I fell a little deeper.

The guys and I had a weekend in December scheduled to surprise her at one of her competitions within driving distance.

I didn't know if they figured out the difference in our relationship immediately or if they simply always assumed it was this way, but nothing had changed. I was both grateful and terrified.

The week of Halloween, TU football had another early game. Stephen texted to remind me of my last foray over there and how I could do better. He was right. Eva came to a lot of my games, so I put in the effort to go to this one.

Timing would be tight with morning skate, but our game didn't start until six. Plenty of time before I had to report to the arena. Even better, Reece and Cole had somehow talked Mase into spending Saturday night at a haunted house party, which meant Eva and I had the house to ourselves after.

I didn't bother Dougie this time since Stephen had sent a ticket with his text. He wasn't subtle, but I was glad he was on my side. If it had been up to Eva, I'd never set foot in the stadium. She was worried someone would figure out we were together, but I pointed out I wouldn't even be within touching distance. As long as she kept the eye fucking to a minimum, we'd be fine.

Eva did *not* back down from a challenge.

I found my seat, directly in front of the TU cheerleaders, where they were once again practicing their partner stunts. Football wasn't my sport, obviously, but I usually enjoyed watching the matchups. Unless my girlfriend was doing crazy tumbling runs in a short skirt with a sassy grin on her face.

The game could have been played by the marching band and I wouldn't have noticed.

In the final minute of the second quarter, TU was pushing for a touchdown, and Eva nodded at her partner, Leon. He grabbed her waist and popped her up above his head, holding her with one hand. Eva smiled and waved for the crowd to cheer louder.

I shifted back and forth between watching the action on the field, hoping for another score to put us up by ten, and watching Eva, who could probably do this stunt in her sleep. Out of the corner of my eye, I saw the angry girl from their practice—Juliet—gesture violently toward Eva's group while talking to an older woman.

The kicking team warmed up behind them, but I didn't take my eyes off Juliet. She looked like she was about to cause trouble. The older woman, probably their coach, shook her head and walked toward the football players on the sidelines.

Juliet frowned and moved forward to say something to the spotter. Eva's partner, Leon, dropped his eyes to the other woman for a second, and Eva wobbled dangerously. I wanted to shout for him to pay attention, but TU scored, making the crowd erupt into cheers.

Eva's jaw clenched as she fought to stay upright, but Leon was moving too much trying to find his balance again. Juliet stepped closer, directly into his path, waving her arms wildly as she appeared to berate the spotter.

I watched my girl realize the second she was going to fall. She shouted to Leon, but it was too late. He popped her out of his hold, and she went sideways. Only her extreme core strength kept her anywhere near him. Unfortunately, Juliet was directly under Eva.

Leon tried to catch her, to the extent that he bulldozed Juliet right into the spotter, but he only managed to get one arm under her. Juliet shrieked as one of Eva's legs caught her in the face, and the spotter tried to shove past in a lopsided dive.

My heart jumped into my throat when Eva hit the

ground, and I reacted, vaulting over the railing to get down to the field. Only a few of the fans around me had noticed her fall, but my acrobatics drew the attention of the crowd.

I didn't think—I only needed to get to her.

Eva and the two male cheerleaders were a tangle of limbs. Juliet had already backed away holding her nose. I heaved the spotter up and got my first good look at Eva. She was curled in a ball, half on top of Leon, eyes clenched shut, holding her shoulder.

I crouched next to her. "Eva?"

She cracked one eye open and sent me a pained smile. "Just a second. Knocked the wind out of me."

Leon apologized over and over until she smacked his thigh. "Stop. It's not your fault I fell. You kept me from hitting the ground. Mostly." He apologized one more time, despite her warning.

Eva shook her head and rolled to a sitting position. "Go get Coach Kat, will you?" He nodded and took off toward the group of football players.

The tightness in my chest eased as she made a joke with the other cheerleaders who'd stayed to help, albeit with a shadow of pain in her eyes. The sight of her falling would haunt me, and I was holding myself back by a thread from simply carting her out of there. I knew what it was like to take a hit. She'd be sore at the very least.

I caught her chin, checking her pupils, but not finding anything out of the ordinary. "Did you hit your head?"

"Not really. My shoulder took the brunt of it."

Whistles blew, and the football teams slowly started leaving the field for halftime, but a man I recognized sprinted toward us from the TU bench. He'd left his helmet behind, and his eyes were locked onto Eva.

"Girl, you okay?" He sounded as panicked as I probably

had, and several other players along with her coach followed him at a slower pace.

She gently pulled away from my hand to face him. "I'm fine. Hazards of the sport."

He knelt next to her, his dark eyes flicking over me before searching her for injuries. "Don't lie to me. Leon ran over there and said he dropped you."

"And he caught me. I'm fine."

"I'm not leaving until Kat looks you over."

"Mac," she ground out. "Get your ass to the locker room."

The argument died when her coach finally reached us and crouched down next to Eva. "How bad?"

Eva glared at Mac while she answered. "Minor. I landed on my shoulder, and my head bumped the ground."

She tsked. "Dizziness? Nausea?"

"No and no."

Coach Kat nodded. "You're done for today. Do you think you need to go to the hospital?"

Eva straightened her shoulders then winced. "No. I can take care of it at home."

"Like hell you will," Mac shouted.

Coach Kat chuckled and patted his back. "She's had much worse, Mac. She knows her own body. If she was hurt, she'd tell us."

Mac shrugged her off. "I'll go with you to the hospital."

"No. You're going to go join the rest of your team in the locker room, finish your game, and I'll text you an update after you guys have won."

His face closed down. "No chance. I'm taking you to the hospital, Wildcat. Shaw has RJ for the second half, he doesn't need me too."

Eva sighed and met my eyes. "Can you help me up?"

I knew what she wanted from me. Mac wouldn't back down if he thought she was on her own, and I sure as hell wasn't going to leave her side any time soon. Instead of helping her stand, I scooped her into my arms.

I met Mac's worried eyes. "I've got her."

His brows rose as realization washed over him, and I wondered who else was coming to the same realization. With her shoulder tight against me, I tried to stand without jostling her. Eva hissed and burrowed her face into my chest.

Leon reached like he wanted to help, but I swiveled away from him. "I've got her," I repeated.

No one else was touching her.

Eva raised her head with a wince. "Gavin, stop growling at people and get me out of here."

I TOOK HER HOME. On the way there, her coach sent her a text with instructions.

> Coach: Eight hours of observation, if you still have no signs of a concussion, you can sleep and/or resume light activities. I'll have the trainer look you over at the next practice. Rest until then.

I felt like she was a little blasé about one of her athletes getting injured, but she wasn't my coach. Cheer wasn't my sport. For all I knew, falls like that were normal, though I doubted it based on Mac's reaction.

Cole echoed my concerns after depositing Henry next to Eva. "Why isn't she at the hospital?"

Reece draped a throw blanket from... somewhere... over

her shoulders then met us in the kitchen. "Yeah. Isn't someone supposed to be watching her in case she passes out or something?"

Eva piped up from the couch. "*She* can hear you, asses."

I smiled at the arm she threw up flipping all of us off. "I'm watching her."

Cole frowned. "What about pregame?"

"I'll stretch here. The pregame is optional, and I got my time in this morning."

"What about the actual game?" Reece asked with his eyes on Eva.

"By the time I have to leave, Mac will be done playing. He'll sit with her while I'm gone." I hadn't organized that part yet, but I had no doubt he'd be willing. "Go on. I'll meet you at the rink."

We were taking separate cars because they were leaving directly from the game to go to the party. I'd planned to spend my free time before the game with Eva anyway, but I was still a little unsteady from those couple of seconds of fear before I'd seen her grimace up at me. The thought of losing Eva tore me up, and I was having trouble settling the panic.

Reece hollered for Mase down the basement stairs, and all three of them touched Eva's head on their way past, like some kind of good luck charm. Hockey players were a crazy superstitious bunch, but I was in that group too. After they'd left, I brushed Eva's hair as I walked around to join her on the couch.

I opened my arms, and she crawled right into them, laying her head on my shoulder. "Are you sure you don't want to have a medical professional look at you?"

"No," she mumbled. "The pain is already going away, and my head stopped hurting before we even got home."

I stroked her back, trying to find the right way to put my chaotic thoughts into words. "You scared me."

She laughed. "It was pretty scary for me too. If Leon hadn't gotten his arm under me, it would have been much worse."

"I can stay," I said quietly.

Eva sat up to study my face. "You'd skip your hockey game?"

I nodded, tracing her jaw with my knuckles.

She turned to kiss my fingers. "No. Don't let this slow down your momentum. You need to go out on the ice and show Dallas why they drafted you. It's only a couple of hours."

"How would you feel about Mac coming over?"

"Like I don't have a choice, but I'm fine with it. Mac is stubborn. I think seeing me will help him get the urge to cart me to a doctor out of his system."

"What about my system?"

Eva scooted closer, dropping a soft kiss on my jaw. "I have other ways to get it out of your system."

I turned my head to kiss her properly, pouring all the fear and relief coursing through me into showing her how much she meant to me. When she reached for my waistband, though, I caught her hand and pressed it flat.

"Eight hours, Princess. Nothing strenuous for eight hours."

She pouted and dropped her head back down. "What are we supposed to do until then?"

I brushed my lips over the top of her head. "I have three hours until I need to leave for the arena, and I don't plan on letting you go until the last possible second. Pick two movies."

Henry chittered from the nest of pillows she'd made on the far side of the couch, which I took for agreement.

EVA AND MAC both texted me during the game, reassuring me she was fine. Part of me hated the idea I had to get someone else to be there for her, but I remembered Mac's determined expression. He was going to come straight to her after the game anyway. This way, I gave him some time alone with her to deal with the fear.

Cole and Reece took my word on Eva's condition, but Mase frowned at me. "I can help if you need it."

"I thought you despised Eva."

Mase huffed. "I don't despise her specifically. I hate all of you equally. She really going to be okay?"

"If she wasn't, I wouldn't be here."

He nodded, glanced over at Reece and Cole, then sighed. "Don't have sex in my bed."

"Don't come home early," I said to his retreating back.

He lifted a hand and flipped me off. Good enough. Eva was waiting for me at home, and we had one more hour before she cleared protocol.

24

Gavin

Eva was sitting on the couch exactly where I left her. The kitchen was clean, the dishwasher was running, and the house smelled like garlic bread.

I brushed my lips across her temple on the way to drop off my bag outside and came back to face my grinning girlfriend. "You were supposed to rest while I was gone."

She tilted her head up for a real kiss. "I did. Mac made spaghetti and cleaned the kitchen when it ended up being a huge mess. He left a plate for you in the microwave."

Spaghetti sounded fabulous, and the scent of the garlic bread was making my stomach growl. I was always hungry after a game, but in this case, I wanted Eva more than a meal. I leaned down, bracing an arm on either side of her on the back of the couch to get better access to her mouth. When all I did was tease her, she grabbed a handful of my shirt and hauled me closer.

"Go eat," she murmured against my lips.

I pulled back reluctantly, and she gave me a light push. "You need the fuel. Cole texted you guys won the game.

That makes eight in a row for an undefeated season so far. Sounds to me like I'm good luck."

She didn't know the half of it. My stats this season were incredible, and Reece and Cole were on fire. Mase didn't let shit past him. The other lines were gelling, and everyone felt the underlying excitement. We'd started the season with a good bid for the championships, but if we kept playing this way, we were a lock.

I caught her hand and kissed her fingers before heading into the kitchen. "Guess you'll have to keep coming to the games then."

Eva snorted. "And ruin my reputation for being a football girlie?"

"One day, we'll convert you to the dark side." The plate in the microwave was still warm, so I took a bite and groaned. "Is Mac looking for a side hustle? I got used to having someone else do all the cooking and cleaning."

She laughed. "Mac can *only* make breakfast and spaghetti, and as far as I know, the only person he cleans for is his girlfriend, Blue."

A tiny part of me unclenched at the news of Mac's girlfriend. I knew he was one of Eva's oldest friends, but not too long ago, he'd been the one sharing her bed. He'd bolted for her when she'd been hurt, just like me, but he'd let me take her without argument. I had to respect his restraint because he wouldn't have stopped me, but fighting with him would have made the situation worse.

I cleared the plate in minutes and set it in the sink, thinking about the cause of Eva's fall. "Did Juliet apologize?"

Eva followed my train of thought easily, and her face clouded as I joined her on the couch.

"Fucking Juliet," she spit out. "She's a hazard to the team. Coach Kat let me know Leon told her what happened, and she suspended Juliet temporarily while she investigated."

"Is this going to affect your competition team?"

She sighed. "Unfortunately, yes, but we have time before our first competition to change the routines if we have to. On the plus side, I managed to kick her in the face on the way down, so I feel pretty good about that."

"Did we make it onto social media?"

Eva frowned. "Not really. Someone got photos of you, Mac, and Coach Kat crouching around me, but there was only mild speculation about why you'd be down there. I did find one video that caught you jumping down to the field in the background though. You're lucky security didn't kick you out immediately."

"I know most of the security guys, and I wasn't about to sit in the stands while you were injured."

She cuddled closer. "I'm going to remind you I can take care of myself, but it was a pretty sexy jump."

I hated being concerned about who saw me rush to her side. I hated not being able to hold her hand in public or kiss her when she met me after a game. Most of all, I hated that she was okay with it.

Her mouth pressed against my neck, and my cock jumped to attention. Eva had always had this effect on me, one of the reasons I distrusted her so much at the beginning. A relationship with her, even one only based on sex, seemed too dangerous when she wouldn't take it seriously. Now, I couldn't imagine my life without her, but I still wasn't entirely sure where I rated on her priorities.

Honestly, I wasn't sure I cared. She dropped her guard with me, let me get to know the person she was, the person she wanted to be, and I wanted her any way I could get her. Even if she broke my heart in the end.

I blew out a breath, resisting the urge to follow her lead. "You're not distracting me with sex."

She pulled back with a frustrated sigh. "Fine, then we should talk about Danny."

"You want to talk about Danny *now*?"

"Well, I'm awake and not getting fucked, so I might as well make good use of my time."

I would *much* rather spend the evening fucking her than talking about Danny. "They said eight hours, Princess."

"My head doesn't even hurt, Gavin."

"Talk. You have twenty-one minutes left to fill." I set a timer on my phone and put it on the side table before scooting under the blanket with her.

She twisted her lips, and I braced myself for bad news. "I know about the switching, not just at Wildcat. His classes too."

I didn't react the way she clearly expected me to—I laughed. "I'm surprised it took you this long."

She frowned. "Why are you risking everything to show up for classes he's perfectly capable of handling himself?"

I tucked a loose strand of pink hair behind her ear and traced the edge of her jaw with my thumb. "It's not everything. When Danny looks back on this, I want him to know I didn't give up on him. TU has been a godsend, but if everything crashes and burns, I can find another way. I can't find another brother."

"Even if he's being a little shit?"

I smiled, happy she was offended on my behalf. "It's nice knowing I'm the good twin."

She poked me in the side. "Ha ha. Why don't you fight for what *you* want?"

"Why don't you? Your parents get to dictate your future, and you agree to it."

Eva leaned back with a frown. "I don't. They dictate my present to a certain extent, but if they got to pick my future, I'd already be married to a trust fund baby and joining my mom on her charity boards, instead of fucking my roommate in our living room."

"Roommate?" The happiness from a moment ago faded, and the roots of unease I'd been ignoring suddenly bloomed large.

Her jaw firmed, and she doubled down. "You *are* my roommate."

"Cole is your roommate. Reece and Mase, they're your roommates. I'm the one you sleep with every night. The one you text when you had a good day or you want to vent. I'm the one who brings you coffee in the courtyard when you're running late for your Tuesday date with Stephen. Try again, Princess, because roommate doesn't cover it."

"Boyfriend? Lover? Sugar boo? If you know what you are to me, why does it matter what word I use?"

Hurt sliced through me. "Because I'm not sure *you* know what I am to you. If you can't even admit it here, when we're alone, what am I supposed to think?"

Eva wet her lips and looked down at her lap for a long second. The sad part was no matter what she said, I wouldn't leave. I'd sit there and take whatever crumbs she offered me. I braced myself for her to tear me down, but she gave her head a shake and met my eyes with determination.

"You're right. I'm starting a fight because when I got hurt, all I wanted was you. Depending on another person to be your strength is a dangerous habit—one I've avoided until now. But I wanted you, and there you were." She reached for my hand, linking our fingers together. "I *do* know what you mean to me. I've never needed anyone else the way I need you."

The bruise softened and faded. Eva held my gaze as her admission charged the air between us. I wanted to be her strength. She was scared, the same as me, by the intensity of her feelings, but I wouldn't hurt her. The only thing I could do was show her and give her time.

I lifted her hand to kiss her fingers. "You have me."

My phone beeped from the table, and her lips curled into a slow smile. "Time's up."

I threw the blanket back, tossing it somewhere behind the couch. "If anything hurts at all, you tell me to stop."

She grinned. "If it doesn't hurt a little, you're not doing it right."

Tonight wasn't going to be soft and gentle. My emotions were too close to the surface, and I knew I wouldn't be able to stop myself from demanding everything. She needed me, but I needed her too.

I fisted my hand in her hair and tilted her head to the side, giving me access. "I've fantasized about this since the first time I found you in here with Reece and Cole."

She gasped as I sucked hard on her neck, fully intending to leave a mark. "Oh really? I had no idea you fantasized about them. Hot."

"That fucking mouth of yours," I muttered, letting her go for a second so I could stand and unbutton my jeans. "Come here."

Her eyes gleamed as she grinned at me and licked her lips. "Which one are you imagining me as—Reece or Cole?"

"On your knees, Princess." I didn't expect her to obey, not at first, and she didn't disappoint.

Eva leaned back against the couch and raised a brow. "Make me."

I quickly stripped naked, then straddled her legs, leaning over her to brace myself on the couch. Eva's eyes dropped to my cock, bobbing between us, but she didn't engage. I leaned in to graze my lips along her cheek.

"I don't have to make you. You're going to beg for it. I'm going to fuck your sassy mouth until your throat remembers the shape of me, then I'm going to make you come on my tongue until my name is the only one on your lips."

Her eyelids fluttered at my words, and she reached for me, but I tipped my hips back. "I'm hard for *you*, Eva. Always you." I pressed a kiss to her neck, knowing I had her when she let her head fall to the side.

Eva was sharp and beautiful and confident, but in the end, she always surrendered to me.

"On your knees," I growled into her ear, then pushed away from the couch to stand again.

She met my eyes, then slowly slid to the floor.

"Lose the clothes," I ordered.

Eva quickly shed the tank top and sweats she'd changed into when we got home, leaving her naked at my feet. I stroked myself a few times then tipped her chin up with my free hand.

"Open for me."

She didn't hesitate. Over the last few weeks, we'd tried every position imaginable, and this was by far one of my favorites. Eva's ice blue eyes looking up at me with her lips wrapped around my cock. She licked and sucked, knowing exactly how I liked it, while I fought to stay standing under the onslaught.

I trailed a finger down her cheek. "Touch yourself. Show me how much you like having my cock in your mouth."

Her hand disappeared between her legs, and a whimper vibrated the back of her throat. I wrapped her hair around my fist, and she let me take control. Her nails dug into the backs of my thighs, urging me on as I thrust into her mouth.

A tingle started at the base of my spine, and I pulled out, not ready to be done yet.

"Ass on the couch, Princess. It's my turn."

She scrambled up, and I pulled her thighs forward, running my thumbs up the inside of her legs to coax her wider. I dreamed of her like this. Spread out before me, desperate hands gripped in my hair, her taste on my tongue.

Over and over again, I brought her to the brink only to ease off right before she could climax.

"Please, Gavin," she gasped.

I chuckled against her wet heat. "You begged so nicely, but the thing is, Princess, I decide when you're done."

Eva's eyes narrowed dangerously, but she uttered a quiet *fuck* when I added another finger, this time to her ass. It never failed to get her off, and within minutes, she was bucking under me. I withdrew my fingers from her, where she'd been squeezing me tight, and rolled on the condom I'd stashed in the pocket of my jeans earlier.

I curled an arm under her limp form and sat on the couch, lifting her onto my lap. She kissed me, and I let her slow things down, savoring the way her mouth moved against mine. Eva made a greedy noise and rolled her hips.

"Need you," she murmured.

"I'm yours," I whispered back. "Take what you need."

She lined me up with her entrance and sank down slowly until I was buried to the hilt. I pressed my thumb against her clit while she moved and gripped her ass hard enough to leave bruises in the shape of my fingerprints.

"That's it, baby. Ride me."

I licked at her pebbled nipples, sucking one into my mouth then the other while she went wild, head tossed back, muttering incoherent curses. Eva was stunning when she fully let go, and my heart stuttered in my chest. She came again, and when her movement slowed, I gripped her hips and thrust upward, chasing my own release.

After cleaning us both up, I carried her to my bed. Sex in the living room was fun, but the couch wasn't even big enough for me, let alone two of us. Eva immediately curled up against my side and fell asleep, but I stayed awake for a long time after with the future on my mind.

25

Eva

I usually loved Halloween. Coming up with a group costume for my crew of football players—and now their girlfriends—should have been the highlight of my semester, but this year, all I wanted was to spend the night with Gavin.

Not even naked. No, I wasn't looking forward to several hours with his dirty, dirty mouth, though I was hoping we'd also get to the naked time. I was going out with a group of hockey players I barely knew because Gavin couldn't say no, and apparently, neither could I.

He'd officially ruined me, but first, I had practice and a meeting with Carl to endure.

The sun beat down as I walked from my car to practice, but the wind brought a distinct chill perfect for Halloween. I was glad for the cooler weather because I had bruises all over me along with a fading hickey on my neck thanks to my boyfriend, the hockey asshole. I could get away with a high neck sweater and full-length leggings since I wouldn't be doing anything active today.

Earlier, the athletic trainer had raised his brows when he

spotted the perfect fingerprints on my ass to go along with the purple splotch on my hip from the fall. He didn't say anything about it though, simply advised I wait a few more days until I resume full activities since my shoulder still felt a little sore.

I didn't bother telling him I'd resumed my *activities* almost immediately. Gavin had barely let me out of his sight —or his bed—the last two days. I came to practice today because with Juliet suspended from the team, I was the sole remaining captain of our squad.

I smiled on my way up the steps. If I'd known I needed to take a dive to get rid of her, I might have tried it earlier. The memory of Leon's horrified face right after the fall took away most of my petty joy. Coach Kat met me at the door to the gym, and I handed her the report from the trainer.

She read it and sent me a knowing look. "No flying or tumbling until your shoulder is one hundred percent."

I nodded, not willing to make anything worse. "I know. I'm here to help and work on the choreo."

"Okay. Leon is a mess. Maybe you could talk to him."

Behind her, I could see the various stunt groups standing around chatting, but I didn't spot Leon. "Where is he?"

She pursed her lips. "In his car."

I sighed. "I'll take care of it."

"One more thing," she stopped me before I could turn around and retrace my steps to the parking lot. "I know you and Juliet weren't on the best of terms, but she's claiming you kicked her on purpose. Any response to that?"

Several responses flew through my mind, none I could say out loud to my coach. "I was trying not to land on my head. I didn't even know she was underneath me until I hit her on the way down." It wasn't entirely the truth because I could hear her yelling at James, our spotter, but I didn't know exactly where she was standing since she was slightly behind me.

Coach Kat nodded. "That's what I expected you to say. There's enough video of the incident that I feel confident in my choice to suspend her. By the way, next time tell your hero to use the stairs. We don't need another student injured. I'll start warmups."

She rubbed my arm and blew her whistle for the group while I trudged back outside. It took me almost an hour of a heart to heart with Leon to get him to come back to practice. I'd fallen plenty of times before in my cheer career—and in ice skating and gymnastics before that—but Leon had never dealt with his flyer hitting the ground.

Once we were inside, practice ran smoothly. Without Juliet there causing problems and questioning every decision, we were finally able to get through a good portion of the routine. I was feeling good about the progress when I walked into Carl's office after lunch.

At some point during practice, I'd ditched the sweater for my tank top, and the weather had warmed up enough outside I didn't think about putting it back on. At least, not until Carl turned to look at me and raised a brow.

"I heard you'd had a fall, but I was unaware you injured your neck."

My hand started to rise to cover the hickey from Gavin, but I forced it back down and raised my chin. "I didn't. It's from a separate incident."

I showed my teeth in a sharp smile, daring him to ask about my sex life, but as usual, Carl left it at the single passive aggressive comment.

He sent me a bland look and leaned back in his chair, crossing his hands over his stomach. "You've done good work so far this semester. I think it's time we added another component to the assistantship."

I resisted the urge to roll my eyes. The work I'd done this semester was entry level at best. I'd nailed it, of course, but it hadn't exactly been challenging.

"What do you have in mind?"

"A job offer."

Shock froze me in place for a couple of long beats. Carl gave me a smug smile, like he enjoyed having the upper hand for once. He hadn't offered jobs to the other assistants directly. They'd had to go through the hiring process, and they worked under a different supervisor to keep things at least superficially fair.

Why would he offer me a job when he hadn't tested any of my skills, let alone taught me anything about the way he ran his business?

I took a slow breath to gather my thoughts and make sure the suspicion didn't show on my face. "I'm happy to discuss an offer, but I haven't completed any projects for you. I've only provided background research."

He shifted side to side slightly, watching me. "Obviously, the job wouldn't begin until you graduated. I wouldn't want to take too much time away from your studies, but I believe you have the appropriate qualifications for a position I have in mind."

His vague response set off all kinds of warning bells. If he reached for his pants, I was out, and he'd be hearing from my lawyer.

"What position would that be?"

"Senior coordinator for social media management."

My eyes narrowed—that was a management position I was definitely *not* qualified for. "And what do you want in return?"

"I'd like for you to act as my personal assistant for the remainder of your contract in addition to the aforementioned duties. Take care of my calendar, schedule meetings, accompany me to events."

It was the last one he really wanted. His hands tightened on each other, and his voice deepened very slightly. Why would he want to—

The truth hit me from a far-fetched connection in my head. I'd suspected I'd gotten the assistantship due to my father's name, but I hadn't considered he might be using me for access. Carl had made it sound like he knew my dad when he first congratulated me on winning the spot.

Invitations for my dad's political fundraiser had recently gone out, and I was almost certain Carl wasn't on the list.

"Let me be sure I understand you correctly. You'll offer me a job I couldn't hope to get anywhere else as a new graduate, and in return, I'll take you with me to my father's fundraiser as my plus one. What's the matter? Couldn't get tickets on your own?"

His amusement faded. "Your father only invited a select group of people. As my assistant, it wouldn't be strange for you to show up with your boss."

I shook my head slowly. "Sorry, Carl. My dad already has my dance card filled with prospective dates. He's not interested in a prospective boss."

Carl rubbed his smooth chin, dropping the pompous attitude a bit. "Take me as your date, then."

I stood, immediately done. "I regret to inform you I have to resign from the assistantship. Thank you for your time."

He spoke before I could take a step. "The job offer is real, but the date won't be. You're very attractive, but unfortunately, not my type." He spun around the single picture on his desk, revealing him and another guy in hiking gear with big smiles on their faces.

I'd noticed the picture before, but I'd assumed the other guy was a friend. With the current context, my view shifted drastically. My frown deepened. I wished the business world didn't care who was fucking who, but he'd been painted as a bit of a playboy, with one beautiful woman after the next on his arm for social events.

He may not have much respect for my skills, but I was good at digging up information. Nobody knew Carl Bennington was gay. I wasn't sure why he was hiding it at this point, but it was his life. At least he wasn't hitting on me.

I slowly sank back into my chair. Carl would probably pass muster with my dad, meaning I'd be able to bring him if I asked, but I didn't want a job offer based on my family line. This was also the second time I'd been placated with my looks, as if I didn't own a mirror.

"Why do you want access?" I assumed the usual, but I wasn't about to bring in a psycho who wanted to hurt my family.

"The same reason everyone else is there. Networking. That ballroom will be filled with people who could benefit my business, and the hard-to-come-by tickets will make it even more useful. Everyone there will assume everyone else there is worth their time to talk to."

I had a sudden appreciation for how Carl had become such a success in the business world, and my frustration at his refusal to teach me anything grew. The job offer was tempting, but I balked at the idea I hadn't earned it. I *would* earn it, in time, though this felt like cheating.

"I need to think about it."

Carl nodded. "Let me know what you decide. In the meantime, I hope you'll continue the assistantship."

I let out a laugh. "Do you really? Because you're not making use of my talents. I'm not interested in being a glorified secretary. Give me a challenge or find another assistant."

He tilted his head in assent. "I'll look through my files."

With nothing else to discuss, I left. The guys were at practice, so I'd have the house to myself, but I didn't head home immediately. Henry would be fine a little longer, and I needed advice.

26

Eva

The courtyard next to Wildcat had lost the riot of color from the late summer blossoms, but the quiet and stillness seeped into me all the same. I sat on the edge of the fountain and tilted my face up to the sun, closing my eyes to let my thoughts chase each other in circles.

Carl's offer was tempting from a purely logical standpoint. I wanted to achieve a high-level job with a successful company, and I could have it. All I had to do was trade my principles for introductions. Did the position mean anything if I didn't earn it?

Did the position mean anything anyway? I was starting to doubt my rock-solid plan for the future, and I didn't like the feeling of being untethered. Before I could travel any farther down that road, I called Stephen. He answered immediately, and my entire body relaxed.

"Do you have a couple of minutes?"

Stephen set something aside and turned his desk chair so I could see out the high-rise window behind him. "I'll always make time for you, sweet cheeks. What's up?"

"You remember the fundraiser my dad is forcing me to attend so he can prove he's a family man?"

"Yes?" Stephen drew the word out into a question.

"Carl Bennington wants me to take him as my date."

His eyes widened. "Your professor? Does he still have both balls?"

"Apparently, he's not interested in me. He wants access to my father's cronies." I paused, still a little stunned at the events of the meeting. "Stephen, he offered me a job."

He sniffed. "About time he did something right."

I sighed. "No. He offered me a job in exchange for taking him as my date."

"Oooh," his lips stayed in an O while he considered, then he tilted his head. "Is it a good job or a low-ball offer?"

I laughed. "A good job. One I'm not actually qualified for."

Stephen waved the evaluation away. "You'll grow into it."

"Thank you for your unwavering support, as misplaced as it is, but I feel uncomfortable with the deal. I recognize that I come from a place of privilege, but I want to earn my spot."

"What does Gavin have to say about you pimping out your plus one for a work opportunity?"

Guilt skittered down my back and settled in my stomach like a rock. "He doesn't know."

"About Carl the creep?"

"About any of it. Well, he knows who Carl is, but I haven't told him about the senate run or the fundraiser yet. I can't risk my dad finding out about us."

For the second time in five minutes, Stephen's eyes widened. "Girl, what are you doing?"

"He knew about my dad's deal before he got involved. I

told him we'd have to keep any relationship a secret and he agreed." I leaned forward. "He *agreed*."

Stephen looked at something off the screen for a second, then back at me. "How much does he mean to you? For real. He's a good guy, and even I'm starting to wonder if you're just playing with him."

A shot of hurt made me sit up straight. "Are you on his side now?"

"There shouldn't be sides, Eva. There should be you and him working together to get through the hard stuff. Does he make you happy?"

"Yes." No question. Just thinking about Gavin caused a flutter in my chest.

"I know you make him happy. I've seen the way he stares at you like he can't see anything else."

The flutter turned into an entire field of butterflies. "There's more to a relationship than endorphins."

He raised a brow. "Oh yeah. Please tell me more about relationships, Miss I Don't Date. How about this? Look me in my face and tell me you aren't in love with him."

I tried to look him in his face and chickened out. "This is stupid."

"I knew it," he said softly. "You're in love with him. I know it's scary for you—it's scary for everyone—but you have to talk to him, trust him."

"I do trust him."

"Then why are you keeping him a secret?"

I dropped my head back. "Stephen, I'm one semester away from graduating. You know my dad wouldn't hesitate to cut me off. What am I supposed to do? Beg Gavin to take care of me?"

Stephen's hands flew up. "Yes. Life gets hard, and you take care of each other. If daddy dearest does cut you off, ask for help. I have money. Your football friends have money. Hell, two of them play in the NFL now. I'll bet they could float you enough to get you through one semester of college."

"I refuse to be a burden to anyone."

He sighed, deep and dramatic. "You. Are. Not. A. Burden. Asking for help is not a sign of weakness. And loving someone doesn't have to be hard. Take Gavin to the fundraiser. Tell your dad the truth. You love your hockey hottie, and you won't be dating anyone else. I know it's what you want to do, or you wouldn't have called me."

Tears welled up in my eyes, and I sniffled. I hated the idea of the fundraiser. Hated the dress my parents had picked out. Hated the sit still look pretty etiquette they'd expect. Hated that I couldn't show off my sexy, talented, wildly kind boyfriend to the people who were supposed to love me the most.

I hated Brendan would never get to meet him.

If Gavin were there, I wouldn't hate it. We could secretly mock the stuffy attendees and eat too many fancy hors d'oeuvres and maybe I'd drag him into a back room so he could steal my panties again. He'd make the fundraiser fun. And under it all, I wanted him to hold me and whisper 'Princess' in my ear and never let go.

Fuck. Stephen was right. I needed to talk to Gavin.

He nodded when I met his eyes. "Good girl."

I let out a wet laugh. "Please don't ever say that to me again."

"Not my fault Gavin's dick has melted your brain." He pursed his lips in thought. "Honestly, I'm not at all surprised. His friend Reece could melt my—"

"Stop," I begged. "Please stop. I have to live with Reece. I don't want to know what he's doing with his dick."

"There she is. Go forth and grab happiness by the balls."

I wiped away the wetness under my eyes. "Do good in the world."

He grinned. "And don't take shit from anyone. Not even your parents—and especially not yourself."

"Love you."

"Love you too, sweet cheeks." He hung up, and I realized I needed to move or I was going to be late.

I tucked my phone away and headed home. It was so easy to tell Stephen I loved him. He'd been a constant from the day we'd met, and I couldn't imagine my life without him. Why didn't my feelings for him trigger my need to immediately push him away?

Why were my feelings for Gavin so much scarier?

I loved Stephen, like I loved Mac, but what I felt for Gavin was different. If I lost Stephen, it wouldn't destroy me. Hell, I'd walked away from Mac on purpose. I was physically incapable of walking away from Gavin. He owned me, heart and soul. How was I supposed to protect myself when I had no armor left?

I expected to find all four guys waiting for me in the living room, but when I slammed into the house, I only saw Gavin studying on the couch. He lifted his gaze, and my heart contracted.

"Hey, Princess." He grinned, and the usual greeting hit me sideways. My emotions were all over the place, and I blamed Stephen for making me think about my feelings instead of pushing them to the back of my mind.

My steps stuttered, and he stood with a questioning tilt to his head. I'd intended to rush upstairs and change, but suddenly, I needed to feel his arms around me. My bag hit the ground at my feet, and I was airborne. Gavin caught me as if I launched myself at him every time I entered the room.

My legs locked around his waist, my arms around his neck, and his hand tangled in my hair.

His mouth found mine, and I poured myself into kissing him. A rumble came from his chest, and my back hit the wall next to the door. I felt raw and wild and free. Fire blazed through my nerve-endings, burning away the fear.

This. This was why I'd finally fallen. Gavin touched me, and the world disappeared. Scorched to ash and remade as a place where I wasn't alone anymore.

He braced an arm under my ass, holding me up, as he brushed my nose with his. "Everything okay?"

"I'm just happy to see you," I muttered.

He flashed me a smile, then lowered me to the ground as Reece and Cole came clomping down the stairs in their costumes. They looked great as superheroes. I wasn't about to waste the opportunity of putting my highly fit, attractive roommates into spandex bodysuits.

Reece pouted. "You're not in your costume?"

"I know I'm late. I only need like ten minutes."

Cole turned to shout as I ran up the stairs. "Henry had her bath time and a fresh diaper. I have Sarah and Duck cued up in my room for her too."

"Dude," Reece muttered.

I didn't hear the rest of what he had to say because I was throwing on a short black sweater, leggings, cat ears, and a tail. My last-minute Catwoman. Technically, Gavin wasn't in his Superman costume either, but he'd flat out refused to wear the tight pants I'd gotten him. His costume was the pared down version of everyone else's, meaning he'd put a tight superman shirt on under an open button down.

Honestly, I was kind of glad. His ass looked fantastic in those pants, and I'd have spent the whole party trying not to mark my territory. After my come to Jesus talk with Stephen, I wasn't so sure I wanted to resist anymore.

My dad had leverage over me, and he lived for control. He'd hate the fact he couldn't make Gavin dance like a puppet. I didn't want to put Gavin in the crosshairs of my father's ire, but I wasn't sure how to keep him out of it while simultaneously claiming him in front of the world.

When I made it back downstairs, the guys were waiting by the door. Casey Jones, Captain America, Deadpool, and my very own Clark Kent. Our group of crime fighters was eclectic. Reece called dibs on Casey Jones, we'd picked Captain America for Cole, and Mase refused to wear any other superhero besides Deadpool. I was just glad they'd agreed to my silly idea.

Reece shook his head. "I still say you would have made a badass Harley Quinn with the pink hair."

I flicked the strands behind my shoulder and met Gavin's appreciative gaze. "Guess I have a thing for cat ears."

He chuckled and opened the door. "Come on. The party already started."

Unlike my usual circuit of Greek parties, this one didn't feature too many football players. We'd arrived in the same neighborhood as Kappa house, but to a smaller place with less of a frat vibe. A cheer went up when we walked in, and from the way everyone greeted my roommates, I suspected the entire hockey team was packed into the living room.

The lights were low, the music was loud, and the drinks were plentiful. I circled the space, chatting with people I'd seen maybe once but who acted like we were besties. The perils of a successful social media account. Gavin moved in the opposite direction, always keeping me in his line of sight.

Even when I wasn't facing him, I could feel his gaze on

me. I knew I needed to talk to him about Carl's deal, the fundraiser, my dad's senate ambitions... my growing feelings, but I was highly aware of all the people in the room who could ruin the delicate balance of my life if the wrong photo got out.

Gavin's black-framed glasses didn't hide his face at all, and my painted-on whiskers weren't fooling anyone. By the time our circles collided again, a guy I vaguely recognized was shifting his weight back and forth in front of Gavin like he couldn't stand still.

"Archer Bolme, man. He's going to be here on Friday."

My ears perked up. I knew Archer Bolme. He was on again, off again dating my friend Blue's mom. With all the drama between Blue and Mac and her mom over the summer, I'd forgotten Archer was the coach of Dallas' professional hockey team.

Gavin laid a hand on his friend's shoulder. "Sellers, I'm going to tell you this one more time. Professional coaches don't do their own scouting."

Sellers shrugged Gavin off. "I know. Why aren't you more excited?"

Gavin met my eyes as I approached and heat swept through me. "I'm excited. Carter already told me he's coming. He wants to talk to me after the game."

Sellers choked on his drink, and Gavin had to pound his back a couple of times. "Breathe, dude. It's not a big deal. Dallas drafted me years ago, remember?"

I frowned, remembering Gavin sharing his frustration about how hands off Dallas had been since he was disqualified from his Juniors championship. Trying to be as casual as possible, I stepped up next to them, careful not to stand too close to Gavin.

"You think you got Dallas' attention again?" I asked.

Gavin smirked at me. "Guess I'll find out on Friday. You coming to the game, Princess?"

Their Friday game was the same night as the fundraiser in Dallas. The one I was supposed to talk to Gavin about attending. Disappointment crushed the hope I'd been carrying since talking to Stephen. I couldn't ask him now. He'd find a way to be there and miss his chance to finally connect with his future team.

I refused to be the reason Gavin risked his dream. "Can't. I have princess things to do. You'll just have to win without me."

Sellers stepped back to take in my outfit. "I would definitely play better if you were there wearing my jersey."

With a growl, Gavin pushed a laughing Sellers toward a group of sexy nurses beckoning him over. The move shifted him toward me, and his hand brushed mine. Tingles shot up my arm from the light touch, and I wondered how soon was too soon to beg for a ride home.

He leaned down, and his breath warmed my ear. "The only jersey you're wearing is mine, Princess."

I shivered at the possessive tone and steeled my resolve. "Not really a jersey type of girl."

Gavin's eyes narrowed at my response, but Reece yelled for him from the kitchen. He raised a brow, and after I nodded for him to go, I pulled out my phone to text Carl. *You have a deal.*

27

Gavin

Something was going on with Eva. Since the Halloween party a couple of days ago, she'd been quieter than usual. She wasn't pushing me away or icing me out, the opposite really, but something in her felt broken.

I'd hoped she'd come to me, talk to me, let me help, but Eva was as fiercely independent as always. Tonight would be the first Friday game she'd miss since we got together, and I wondered if it was connected.

Maybe Danny had done something. Or Juliet. Or her weird professor. I didn't know because she wouldn't talk to me. My money was on Danny since he'd been strangely absent the last few weeks.

Even stranger, after the econ test at the beginning of the semester, Danny hadn't asked me to switch with him. Not for shifts at Wildcat and not for any of his classes. I was getting a little worried, so I detoured to Wildcat after my morning skate. He usually worked game days, and I could bring Eva her favorite coffee.

Danny wasn't inside, and Patrick, one of the nicer guys

who worked there and knew our secret, hadn't seen him around. He hooked me up with a rush order, and I texted Danny while I waited.

> Me: Are you in jail?

> Bro: Ha ha. [laughing emoji]

> Me: Need to talk.

I didn't get a response, but he'd read the message. Danny only ever did what *he* wanted to do, so I didn't expect him to put any effort into communicating. I'd been thinking about our fucked-up situation since Eva had found out, and she was right. Doing the work for Danny wasn't helping him. I was taking the easy route in a relationship I didn't know how to handle.

If I was serious about being there for my brother, we needed to hash some shit out and try for real. Which meant no more stupid risks.

Patrick nodded at me and set my drink on the counter. Iced cold brew with four pumps of vanilla syrup and two sugars. Eva loved her milkshake coffee, and I loved making Eva happy. With the Danny problem temporarily tabled, my mind was split between the game tonight and whether I could convince Eva to be late to practice. I didn't notice the guy walking behind me until he spoke.

"Danny King?"

At my brother's name, I stopped and turned without saying anything. Silence was the best way to keep people guessing.

"Or should I call you Gavin?"

I bristled at his knowing tone. The guy was a couple of inches shorter than me, at least twenty years older if the silver hair at his temple was any indication, and rich. He wore his privilege like a good cologne. His suit looked expensive, and his watch definitely was. I had no idea what he wanted with me, or my brother, until I got a good look at his eyes.

Ice blue and filled with contempt. I knew that expression—Eva had worn it every time our paths crossed for the first two years we'd known each other.

"Mr. Adams," I greeted him. No point in pretending I didn't know who he was.

His mouth curved in a humorless smile. "I'd like a moment of your time."

I was severely tempted to simply say no and keep walking. Somehow, I doubted he'd want to hear I was in a hurry because I wanted to fuck his daughter before she had to leave for practice.

Instead, I inclined my head toward Eva's courtyard. He followed me, and I set the coffee down on the lip of the fountain. I liked to have my hands free when strange men surprised me. My eyes narrowed as I thought about it. How had he even known where I'd be?

Eva's dad gave the space a quick, unimpressed glance then focused on me again. "I'll cut to the chase. I want you to stay away from my daughter."

My brows rose, and I had the crazy urge to laugh, followed by the even crazier urge to tell him to fuck off. He didn't get to dictate who Eva dated. She'd probably castrate me if I told her father to fuck off though. Worse, any response I made confirming we had a relationship could hurt her. As much as it pained me, I feigned ignorance.

"We live in the same house, so I can't do that."

His mouth firmed into a thin line. "I'm aware of your living arrangements. I see her credit card bill every month.

I've also seen this." He pulled his phone out of his pocket and pulled up a video he'd saved.

I watched myself jump over the railing at the football stadium and run to Eva's side. My face wasn't clearly visible in the video, but my body language made it pretty evident I'd take out anyone who stood between me and his daughter. On its own, I could make the case I was worried about my roommate, but when the video ended, he switched it to a close-up photo of Eva in my arms a few minutes later.

She'd curled into my chest, and I remembered thinking I'd give anything to take her pain away. This picture was much more damning than the video. Whoever had taken it had nearly zoomed in on my face. I was staring down at her, and there was no mistaking my expression. Anyone looking at this picture would know I was in love with Eva.

Her dad knew about us—our secret was blown. The one thing she asked of me, and I couldn't deliver.

Finished presenting his evidence, he slid his phone back into the pocket of his suit. "I'll tell you again. Stay away from my daughter."

A flare of hope fought its way through the dread. If he already knew, telling him to fuck off probably wouldn't make things worse. The answer was the same either way.

"No." I met his eyes calmly, despite the anger coursing through me. "I'm not going to stay away from your daughter. Not unless *she* asks me to."

He nodded as if he'd expected that response. "You may not be aware of this, but I value my daughter—and what she represents to me—highly. I'm about to announce my candidacy for the U.S. Senate, and my voters will expect my family to represent the best of themselves. Not associating with a drug-addicted hockey player who will probably cheat on her the moment he gets bored."

My shoulders tightened with the need to strike back, but I kept my arms loose at my sides. "Wherever you got your information is wrong. I don't do drugs, and nothing would make me cheat on your daughter. She's fine, by the way. After her fall."

"She always is." I couldn't quite read his tone, but he didn't sound relieved. "You won't be though. I understand you've been drafted by the Dallas Thunder. I also understand you and your twin brother are astoundingly similar. How do you think your prospective employer would respond to you being expelled from school during your last season for helping your brother cheat?"

I tried not to let my sudden fear show, but my face must have given me away because he smiled.

"Stay away from her, and there's no need for the knowledge to go beyond me. You're better off anyway. She's finally chosen someone suitable as her date for my fundraiser, so I imagine her dalliance with you won't be nearly as appealing after tonight."

He didn't know his daughter at all if he thought a political fundraiser would be appealing to her. It took me a second to realize he was threatening her as much as me. She'd broken their agreement, even if she found someone to appease him.

"Don't take this out on her."

He tilted his head. "Now why would I do that? She's fallen in line, and I've taken care of any outliers."

Me. I was the outlier. This guy was supremely confident his threats would have the desired effect, but I suddenly wasn't as worried about me and Danny. We'd figure it out. Eva would be devastated. She hadn't fallen in line, and as soon as he figured out what she was up to, he'd come for her.

Unless I offered a new deal. One I had no intention of keeping, but the appearance would maintain the status quo long enough for her to finish her last semester.

"Dissolve your deal with her, let her finish her degree, and I'll stay away." It was a desperate attempt, but I had to try.

"My deal with her is none of your concern. Good luck in your game tonight." He turned and strode out of the courtyard as if manipulating his daughter's life was simply one more business meeting.

My hands had closed into fists at some point, so I shook them out, trying not to let the frustration and fear win. There was a *lot* she hadn't told me. The fundraiser, her dad's political career, the date for tonight. No wonder she'd been acting strangely.

I stared at Eva's coffee sitting on the fountain and found myself teetering between two equally terrible choices. Water dripped down the outside of the plastic cup and hit the concrete with a quiet splat. I wanted the choices to be equal, but they weren't.

I'd spent the last four years protecting Danny, but TU wouldn't feel that way if they found out about the tests. Technically, we *had* been cheating, though it didn't feel like it. Danny knew the material or he wouldn't be able to pass the classes.

Luckily, Wildcat didn't give a fuck who worked the shift as long as they had tax information on file.

Eva's dad may know about the switching, but I doubted he could prove it. Unfortunately, this was exactly the type of scandal that could scare Dallas away from signing me. The fallout could be disastrous if he followed through, and I had no reason to believe he'd bluff.

Of course, none of the fallout mattered because I wasn't

going to abandon Eva. Danny, the Dallas team, TU, none of it was as important as her. No one else knew about the test switching, and despite my early reservations, I absolutely believed Eva had kept our secret.

She didn't know we'd been caught, and if I understood Eva's dad correctly, she was attending his political fundraiser tonight. One hundred percent he was going to double down on their agreement, taking away even more of her control.

I grabbed her coffee and yanked my phone from my pocket as I made my way back to my car. Eva didn't answer. In fact, the call went straight to voicemail. I sent a text, but as I suspected would happen, she didn't read it. Fuck. Her dad paid for her phone, and the coincidence wasn't lost on me.

The fundraiser had to be somewhere nearby because I left her in my bed only a couple of hours ago. She had practice today, but not for another twenty-three minutes. I could catch her at home.

I rolled through the two stop signs and thanked the traffic gods for the green light on the way back to the house. If I could warn her, we could figure out a way around her dad's threats. Archer was coming to the game tonight. The last time I'd talked to him, he'd seemed like he cared about his players. Maybe he'd understand the situation if I laid it all out for him.

I didn't need a college degree to play hockey, and Eva didn't need her dad's money to pay for school. We could find a way.

If she was willing to fight.

28

Gavin

Instead of finding Eva asleep in my bed, I found Danny lounging on my couch. When I bolted past him toward the stairs, he stopped me with a few words.

"She's not here."

"Fuck." I detoured to the kitchen to put her coffee in the fridge. "Where is she?"

"Don't know."

With her dad's threats forefront in my mind, I had a pretty good idea. She was getting ready for his big debut.

Danny watched me stomp around the house and frowned. "What's going on? I thought you wanted to talk to me."

"I do, but I need to find Eva." At the sound of my voice, Henry came flapping down the stairs, quacking. I picked her up, and she chittered as she settled down in the crook of my arm. "Where's your mama, huh?"

The couch groaned as Danny got up to join me near the dining table. "Have you tried calling her?"

"Yeah, she's not answering."

He held his phone up, tapping the screen. "Let me try. Maybe she just doesn't want to talk to you."

My eyes narrowed. "Why do you have her phone number?"

"We're friends." He left it at that, and we both listened as the call went straight to voicemail.

Danny put his phone away with a frown. "Is this a danger squid situation or a booty call gone wrong?"

I squinted at him. "Neither. She's not in physical danger, but her dad's about to fuck up her life."

"Can't have that," he muttered. "What do we do next?"

"This isn't why I wanted to talk to you."

"So? I like Eva. She deserves an unfucked life, and if you can't handle it, I'm happy to step up."

I lunged toward him, way too close to the edge my temper, but he held up his hands with a grin. "Just messing with you. Eva wouldn't touch me, despite clearly being the superior twin."

My teeth ground together, and Henry made an unhappy noise at my tight grip. "I'm not sure I want your help."

He clapped my back as he moved past me to sit at the table. "Yes, you do. I'm a delight. Now tell me what's going on."

I gave in, setting Henry on the floor and telling Danny about my encounter with Eva's dad, who hadn't even given me his first name.

Danny whistled when I finished. "Are you sure you want to risk everything for her?"

The chair scraped across the floor as I sat down. "Yes. Are you sure you're okay with me risking everything? It affects both of us."

He frowned. "Obviously, I would prefer not to get kicked out of college in my last year for cheating, but it wouldn't destroy me. Why don't you call her friend? The one with the crush on Reece."

"How do you know about Stephen's crush?"

"We're friends," he repeated.

I wondered how often Eva talked to him. A tiny pinch of jealousy came and went. I trusted Eva, and the more I thought about it, the more I liked the idea of her befriending Danny. I'd tried to stay close to him in my own way, and she'd succeeded where I failed.

When I texted Stephen asking for help, he immediately FaceTimed me. He was grinning and bare-chested in a hot tub.

"Why hello, hockey hottie."

"That's hotties, plural." I turned the camera so he could see both of us. "Stephen, meet Danny." Danny nodded, but otherwise seemed happy to sit and listen.

"You really are identical. So unfair," he sighed. "What's with the bat signal?"

"Is Eva going to her dad's fundraiser tonight?"

His head dropped back with a groan. "I'm going to smother her the next time I stay the night. She was so close."

Sometimes I had trouble following Stephen's drama. "Is that a yes or a no?"

He took a deep breath and faced the camera again. "Since she didn't talk to you, I'm assuming she took the deal?"

"What deal?" I asked through clenched teeth. How much of her life had Eva kept hidden from me?

Stephen climbed out of the water and set the phone next to his towel as he dried off. "The short version is yes. She's coming to the fundraiser tonight at her dad's insistence. Carl the creep…"

He paused and tilted his head at me. "You know about Carl?"

She'd told me that much at least. "Yeah. Useless business dude in charge of her assistantship."

He laughed. "That's the guy. He offered her a full-time management position at his company upon graduation in exchange for taking him tonight as her date. Apparently, even with his business credentials, he couldn't get invited to the event."

"She said yes?"

"He claimed he wasn't interested romantically, and she believed him. I'm not so sure, considering how Eva manages to get everyone to love her, but I haven't met him."

I remembered the way her dad had described her, like an asset instead of a daughter.

"If it's any consolation, when I talked to her earlier, she wasn't happy about the way any of this turned out. I get it. I mean, I'm going to be dressed up in Dallas and wasted on a bunch of upper-class assholes."

"You're going too." A plan clicked together in my head, and I made myself take a ten count and consider the ramifications of my actions. Archer, Coach, and the team were all expecting me to play tonight, but some things were more important than hockey. Chasing after Eva wasn't about warning her so much as showing her she wasn't alone. "Take me with you."

Stephen stopped running the towel over his hair and pointed at the camera. "Yes. I love this. You can be my plus one. I'll call Daryll with a raincheck. He won't care."

I had no idea who Daryll was, but I was glad Stephen seemed enthusiastic. "What do I need to know?"

Before Stephen could answer my question, Danny

gripped my arm. "You have a game tonight. You have a game in front of *Archer Bolme* tonight."

I shook him off. "I know. My choice, remember? Eva's dad—"

"Thomas," Stephen supplied.

"Thomas," I slanted my eyes to the phone in thanks. "Thinks he's won. He's going to do everything he can to make Eva feel small and powerless, so he stays in control. I'm not going to let him do that. Eva is not small or powerless. She's fierce and passionate and fucking formidable."

Both men were silent after my little speech. If they couldn't see the truth, then fuck them too. I got up, leaving my phone propped on the table, and searched my backpack for the memento I'd never told anyone I carried.

I tossed my mom's engagement ring on the table where they could both see it. "She's not alone."

Danny picked up the small gold circle and rubbed the opal in the middle. "I can play for you."

My gaze shot to him. "What?"

His jaw tensed, like he regretted speaking up. "I can play for you. I've been doing some coaching on the side at Greenfield, and I spend time every day running drills. They offered me a part-time position for this kids team. I've been trying it out, lowering my hours at Wildcat. Anyway, I can play."

I ran a hand through my hair, shocked as hell he wasn't as unmotivated as I'd thought. After the fiasco at the championships, he'd never shown any interest in hockey other than giving me shit for my place on the team. What else had I missed?

"I appreciate the offer, man, but there's a big difference between drills and DI hockey."

He nodded tightly. "I was just trying to help."

"I know," I said slowly, "but I think maybe the switching thing isn't actually helping anyone."

Danny let out a sigh. "I thought that might be what you wanted to talk about. Yeah, we're done with that. Eva always gets her way, doesn't she?"

I didn't understand the connection, but he wasn't wrong. Eva always got her way—because she worked her ass off to make things happen. For herself and for all the people she cared about.

Stephen snorted. "I can't imagine your team would appreciate the switch either. I'll send you the info for the fundraiser."

My phone dinged with incoming texts. "Thanks. You're a good friend, Stephen."

He snorted. "I'm the best. One more thing. Do you love her?"

"Yes." Hard stop. Nothing else to say.

He smiled. "Good. See you at seven. Oh, and wear something pretty." Stephen hung up, and I frowned at Danny.

"What the hell do I wear to crash a political fundraiser?"

He frowned. "What does the invitation say?"

I squinted down at the screenshot Stephen had sent me. "Black tie. Shit. I don't own a tux."

Danny crossed his arms and leaned back in his chair. "I do."

Shock froze my brain for a second. "Really?"

A muscle ticked in his jaw, and some of his irreverent attitude faded. "Dad bought it for me right before..." He shrugged. "I was supposed to go to that girl's prom with her. Dad said it was a good investment in my future."

My throat closed at the memory of Dad talking about how important it was to prepare for the future. He'd done that by setting us up with the means to get through college, buy this house, follow our dreams.

Danny's gaze turned distant, and I'd bet he was remembering the same speech. Dad had it memorized. He'd bring it out any time one of us hit a milestone or had a setback. One of the hardest moments for me had been at their funeral when I didn't have Dad there to give the speech about looking to the future when things got hard.

I nudged Danny's leg with my foot. "We've both put on thirty pounds of muscle since then. There's no way the tux still fits."

He shook his head. "I've had it tailored—keeping up with the investment. It'll fit."

His generous offer surprised me, but maybe it shouldn't have. I hadn't really looked at my brother in years. In my mind, he was still the hurt kid who'd lost his parents, just like me, but I wasn't that kid anymore and neither was he.

"Danny—"

He cut me off, tucking his chin into his chest. "I'm sorry. I was... messed up after Mom and Dad died. I didn't know how to deal, and it was easy to take it out on you. I never wanted you to get hurt though. I swear I didn't know I was going to fail that drug test."

"I know. The situation was fucked, all the way around."

Danny nodded. "I missed our life. For a long time, I missed the life we used to have. I felt like I'd lost everything."

I squeezed his shoulder. "I never gave up on you."

"I know. You were my constant through all of it. I treated you like utter shit, and you stood by me. Probably don't deserve you, but I'm glad you're here." He heaved out a breath. "Okay, enough sappy bullshit. We need to grab my tux from storage, and you need to tell the team."

I rubbed my face, fighting the urge to hug my brother. He'd probably punch me if I tried it. "I hope Eva worked her magic on the team or I'm going to have a lot of groveling to do after this."

Danny grinned. "Either way, you're fucked."

"You could be less happy about that."

"No," he said with a satisfied sigh. "No, I really couldn't."

29

Eva

I made a mistake. That phrase, which I hated almost more than 'you're very pretty', played on repeat in my mind as I circled the ballroom full of my dad's rich political allies. Mom was here somewhere, probably following Dad around like a human accessory. The perfect wife to go with his perfect daughter.

He'd have the full collection if his perfect son hadn't died.

Carl had abandoned me to network as soon as we'd entered the room, though I had to give him credit for thanking me and making sure I was okay on my own. As if I didn't have a lifetime of experience with these kinds of parties. He should have seen my debutante ball.

I'd kept an eye out for Stephen, since I knew he'd have gotten an invite as a close friend of the family, but so far, he'd been absent. Not surprising considering Stephen loved an entrance.

As I passed the small cocktail tables for the third time, another one of my mom's committee chairs caught me to exclaim how beautiful I looked. I thanked her, and she patted my arm as if I should be proud of my face.

I was slowly suffocating. The people here didn't look past the surface, not even Carl—*especially* not Carl—and my place in the world felt like it had been made for someone else. Neither of my parents had greeted me, despite not having seen me in months. I wasn't necessarily sad about it, but the lack of effort highlighted a telling distinction between my dad's image of a close family and the reality. No one here cared about me, and I'd left behind the man who did.

Suddenly, I was tired. Of everything. I'd spent the last sixteen years trying to live up to the memory of my brother, to be worthy of the sacrifice he made, but none of this made me happy. These plastic people talking about nothing so they could flash their status symbols at each other.

I looked down at my frothy pink dress and shook my head. A designer dress laid out for me after hours of hair and makeup so I could present the exact right image. Was this what I wanted for my future?

How much was I supposed to give up because Brendan died?

Tonight was a terrible time to come to terms with my past trauma, but uncontrolled panic increased my heart rate and stole my breath. I gulped in air and made a beeline for the bar, requesting a water. After gulping down half the glass, I felt calmer, if not better.

Something inside me had shifted, broken free. I missed Brendan. I missed our life before he died, when my dad read me bedtime stories and my mom didn't talk to me through her assistant. Brendan would never have let them cut me out of their lives if I'd been the one to die.

I didn't want to pretend he didn't exist anymore, and I was done trying to live up to a ghost.

Carl's eyes flicked toward me from his group of middle-aged men, and he gave me a tiny smile. At least someone was getting what they wanted. As much as I wished Gavin was the one smiling at me, I'd never ask him to choose me over his future. I should have chosen him—I should have gone to the game.

They must be getting close to the end of the first period, and I desperately wanted to check the score, maybe send Gavin a good luck text. He wouldn't see it until the first intermission, but I wanted him to know I supported him. Unfortunately, my phone had lost service as soon as I got to the room my dad reserved for me at the hotel.

This wasn't really the college sports crowd, but maybe one of the people willing to stop and offer me marriage advice could give me a score update too. I casually checked the men near me, looking for someone on their phone. My father had ignored me up to this point, but my luck ran out when he spotted me hovering near the buffet.

"Eva," he called from his table at the head of the room.

Plan foiled, I pasted on a smile and made my way to him. "Congratulations, Dad. It's a good turnout tonight."

He hummed in agreement and scanned the crowd. "Carl Bennington was a good choice. Popular among young businessmen, up and coming in Dallas society, and not charismatic enough to outshine you. I would have preferred if he weren't your professor, but he meets my requirements. I'm willing to suspend our agreement if you want to keep dating him, though I ask you to wait until he's no longer in a position to decide your grade—not the right image."

Inside, I recoiled, but I managed to keep the pleasant smile on my face. What a load of bullshit. None of the responses running through my head were appropriate for this conversation.

Dad took a drink and his gaze landed on me. "With that in mind, I have a tour of speaking engagements coming up, and your mom is tied up with her charity responsibilities. I want you to accompany me."

"What?" The word came out sharper than I intended, but he'd surprised me.

"Lower your voice," he said quietly. "There's no need to share our personal lives with those around us."

"You started it," I muttered. "I can't go on tour with you. I have classes and practice."

"Naturally, you'd have to postpone your last semester of college, which you'd have to do anyway without the money for tuition."

I dropped the smile as icy dread sank in my gut. "You said you'd keep paying for my expenses."

He took a sip of his whiskey and tucked his hand into his pocket. "I know you broke the agreement."

I gestured at Carl, shmoozing two tables over. "I brought a Dad-approved date to the event you demanded I attend. How did I break our agreement?"

My father wasn't a cruel man, but he could be cunning. He swirled the amber liquid in his glass letting the questions build in my mind. No doubt, he wanted me to start making excuses for all the ways *I* thought I'd fucked up.

I didn't let his power play work on me despite the growing panic crushing my chest. "Well?"

"You've been involved with Gavin King instead of giving the men I've chosen a fair chance. He didn't deny it when I spoke with him earlier." He gave me disappointed look. "I don't want to cut you off, Eva, but actions have consequences. If you do well on the tour, we can see about finishing the last semester of your degree."

Actions have consequences. Didn't I think the same thing to myself when I started softening toward Gavin? The wave of despair I'd been holding back came crashing down on me. Worst case scenario. He wanted me to give up everything I cared about—cheer, school, my friends, Gavin—to maintain my wealth.

I almost laughed at the nonsense. Now that I was forced to pick, the choice was ridiculously easy. I met my dad's eyes, the same blue as mine, without a shred of doubt.

"Thank you, but I have to decline your generous offer. I'm afraid I don't have the time in my schedule to dedicate to your speaking tour."

The edges of his mouth tipped down. "I want you where I can keep an eye on you."

"No, you don't. You want me where you can control me. I'm done with your games. Nothing I do is ever going to live up to Brendan." Dad winced at his name, but I plowed on. "I won't play the role of dutiful daughter to help you achieve *your* goals. I have other roles that mean more to me—like girlfriend and student and boss cheerleader. You may not approve of me or the direction of my life, but you're not going to stop me."

"Is this the influence of the hockey player?"

I crossed my arms and let my inner voice have free rein. The release felt glorious even if what followed scared the shit out of me. "You wish this was his influence. This choice is all me."

"Gavin is a drug addict and a cheat. I knew he'd try to contact you, which was why I shut off your phone. If you follow this path, I'll have to follow through on our agreement and revoke all payments for your accounts. Are you sure you want to give up your privileged life for him?"

Betrayal cut a hard line. He'd done everything he could to cut me off and force me to the position most advantageous to him. His gaze shifted behind me, but I didn't care of one of his cronies overheard me.

"In a heartbeat. Gavin is kind and generous, and he treats me like a woman instead of a doll. He's a brilliant hockey player, a devoted brother, and a leader to his teammates. I couldn't find a better man if I'd built one myself."

"And I'd never let you deal with this alone." Goosebumps rose on my skin as a familiar arm curled around my waist from behind.

I closed my eyes, absurdly happy to hear Gavin's voice. When I opened them again, my father had drained his whiskey. I leaned back against Gavin's chest, covering his arm with mine, and lifted my chin.

"Do what you have to, Dad. I'll still support you publicly, but I'm staying at TU and I'm choosing Gavin."

His lips pressed together, and he nodded. "I see."

I softened at his stiffness. He was frustrated now, but I hoped one day he'd come to the same realization I did. Control was meaningless without joy. "If you're interested in getting to know the real me instead of the pretty doll you seem to think you birthed, you know how to find me."

Dad buried both his hands in his pockets—his tell for when he felt like he'd lost control of a situation. "Call your mother when you change your mind."

"I won't." I linked my fingers with Gavin and led him away with my head high. No one had noticed the exchange, but I spotted Stephen chatting up the bartender. He lifted two flutes of champagne at my exit. I didn't stop until I'd walked us out of the ballroom and around a corner into a little alcove.

Gavin's arms closed around me the second we were alone, holding me steady as I fell apart. His hand cupped my head, and I let the hot tears fall against his chest.

"Shh, it's going to be okay," he murmured into my hair.

I finally laughed, letting go of the last vestiges of my goals before this point. "I know."

My finances were going to be fucked, but Stephen had been right. I had friends with gobs of money. My car was paid off, my grades were on track for spring graduation, and I hoped my living situation would stay exactly as it was. I didn't know how Gavin had ended up here, besides the obvious interference of Stephen, but I was so very thankful.

His lips brushed my temple. "I am in awe of you."

"I did just spectacularly blow up my life." I took a shuddering breath and eased away to see his face. "I'm sorry I didn't tell you about tonight—I didn't want to get in the way of your future."

Gavin's thumb caressed my jawline. "Eva, you are my future. Nothing else matters."

Warmth filled all the cracks and holes I'd tried to close on my own. I'd lost the life I thought I wanted, but I'd gained one a damn sight better. A future with Gavin sounded fantastic, even if it meant letting go of my rigid control and asking for help.

Stephen would never let me hear the end of this.

30

Gavin

I didn't need her to respond—my pulse still raced from hearing her choose me—but I didn't want her to focus on what she might have lost. Her tears made me want to fix the world for her, and I knew exactly how to pull her out of her whirling thoughts.

"Are you wearing a tiara?" I asked.

Eva sniffled and pressed her lips together. "It goes with the outfit."

I let my gaze trail down the fitted bodice to the cloud of pale pink material flaring out from her hips. "I like your dress."

"Thanks. It has pockets." She deadpanned back. "How did you know where I'd be?"

"Your dad threw Carl in my face as your date tonight, and I realized he was going to ambush you. I wanted you to know you weren't alone, so I called in reinforcements."

She shook her head and smiled. "Stephen. No wonder he looked so smug after he got back from the spa. He loves a juicy statement. I'm going to need a new phone, and a bunch of other stuff."

"Do you think your dad will really cancel your accounts?"

"Yes." She smoothed my lapel, wiping at some of the moisture. "He has to prove his point, and he won't want to miss the chance of me changing my mind once I start slumming it like all you peasants. What did he threaten you with?"

"He said he'd inform the school Danny and I were switching in our classes."

Her brow furrowed. "How the fuck did he find out about that?"

I shrugged, and the last lingering doubts faded away. "We'd gotten lazy about it. Anyone who was paying enough attention in Danny's classes might have noticed. We're pretty sure he can't prove anything though. At worst, he'll cause some drama that Dallas might frown upon."

She tried to shimmy past me. "Let me go. I'm going back in there and ruining his fucking evening."

I held tight, but she was stronger than she looked. "No. Eva, stop squirming. He has no incentive to follow through on his threats. The point was to keep me away from you. Clearly, that plan failed. Even if he's petty enough to try to ruin my life for retribution, he won't change much. Archer is at TU waiting to talk to me tonight, and I'm not going to be there."

"Okay, then fuck my father, and let's get you to the game."

She was beautiful all fired up and willing to take on the world for me. Eva in her natural state was a force to be reckoned with, but I was just as fond of the times when she softened and let me take control.

Damn, I loved this girl.

I'd intended to ease her into the topic, considering her

usual reaction was to run the other way, but after what she'd given up for me tonight, I didn't think she needed time. She just needed a little push.

"You love me," I teased.

A flush raced up her cheeks. "We don't have time to get into this. You might not be able to play in your game, but you can still find Archer if we go now."

I tilted my head with a smug smile. "I'm not leaving until you say the words, Princess."

A tortured groan came out of her. "Is it always going to be like this?"

"God, I hope so."

She licked her lips and surrendered, like she always did for me. "I love you."

I cradled her face and rewarded her with a soft kiss. "See, that wasn't so hard, was it?"

"You are such an ass. Let's go." She tugged away and swatted my shoulder.

"Not so fast, Princess." I yanked her back against me, tangling my hands in her hair and knocking a couple of pins loose. Her breath hitched at my tight grip, and fire lit her eyes. "I'm not done with you."

"Whatever you want, it's yours," she whispered.

"I know. I love you too," I murmured, then devoured her mouth.

The traffic gods were on our side, and we made it to the arena during the second intermission. Eva kissed me and sent me back to the locker room with a promise to find a seat.

A bunch of relieved greetings from the team met me as I

strode inside. Most of the guys were in the process of shoveling in a quick snack, so the sound was somewhat muffled. Cole shook his head and dug some money out of his locker, handing it to Reece.

"About time," Coach muttered. "Get your ass in your gear."

My brows shot up. "You want me to dress?"

"Did I stutter? I didn't change the lineup. You better be warmed up because McCarthy is struggling on first line."

I immediately started removing my tux, causing Sellers to whistle. Normally, I'd wear my underlayer from home, but luckily, I had an extra set in my locker. As I stretched and pulled on my pads, I listened to Coach go over the plan for the third period.

"We're tied at nothing, and UW shouldn't be this much of a challenge for us. Tanner, you're slow off the mark, get your head out of your ass." I grinned as Reece saluted him. "Klasky, your stick handling has been sloppy as hell tonight. Mase, excellent work. Keep it up."

I glanced at Mase, but he had his earbuds in. Fifty-fifty he was even listening.

"King, your personal matter better have been worth it," Coach grumbled.

"It was." I stood up and grabbed my helmet from the shelf in my locker, then addressed my team. "Are we going to let UW come into our house and push us around?"

A chorus of *hell no*'s echoed around me.

"Good, let's win this fucking game."

Cheers erupted, and even Mase smiled. Everyone adjusted their gear, and we tromped back out to the ice. A tightness in my chest eased as I breathed in the cold air. I'd never regret going to Dallas for Eva, but I took a moment to stop and take in the roar of the fans, the familiar clunk of our skates, the absolute certainty I belonged there with my team.

When I looked out at the crowd, my eyes locked with Eva's, sitting in her usual seat with the tiara still perched in her messy hair. As I stared, she grinned and turned, showing me the red jersey she wore over her dress with King stitched across it in black. Seeing her sitting there in front of thousands of people, proudly wearing my name, sent a chill through me.

She blew me a kiss, and everything just clicked. Whatever happened tonight, whatever Archer had to say to me, I'd give the next twenty minutes all I had. Then Eva would get everything after.

I played like a beast, taking chances I never would have considered before, and right before the buzzer, I made a beauty of a nearly blind pass to Cole who scored the only point of the game.

For a regular season game, we celebrated like we'd won the Frozen Four. We didn't even make it into the locker room before the guys were dropping their gear and talking about a party tonight. Coach smiled right along with us until a beautiful girl around my age with dark hair and red lipstick caught up to him near the locker room entrance. She said something quietly, gave him a half smile, then walked back down the tunnel in heeled boots ignoring the chaos.

Coach frowned after her, but I'd had enough drama for one night. She wasn't my business. I glanced at Cole standing next to me, intending to see if they were going out, but his eyes were locked on the girl. Reece yelled for both of us, and Cole shook off whatever spell he'd been under. I waved them off, deciding not to even ask. If they went out, great. If not, Henry would have someone to keep her company because I sure as hell planned to keep Eva busy all night.

Instead of my girlfriend waiting for me when I came out of the locker room twenty-five minutes later, Archer Bolme leaned against the wall at the players' entrance scrolling on his phone. My steps faltered for a split second as my stomach churned. If he was going to drop me, I couldn't do anything else at this point.

I'd played the best hockey of my life this season. If he couldn't see the potential past my history, then fuck him.

"Coach Bolme," I said in greeting.

He straightened, putting his phone away in his pocket so he could hold out a hand. "Gavin King. Good game tonight. They really rallied when you took the ice."

I shook his hand, reassured by the smile I saw lurking on his face. "Thanks. It's nice to see you again."

"Sorry for dropping in without warning, but I wasn't sure I'd be able to make the game. I was hoping to have a chance to talk with you. Do you have time now?"

Eva didn't have a phone, so I couldn't call her and let her know I'd be late. When I hesitated, Archer held up his hands. "No pressure if you have somewhere else to be. I know how nerve-wracking this process can be, but I'm not about to crush your dreams. We're excited to welcome you in Dallas. I think you'll be an asset to the team."

I tilted my head, trying not to let the wave of relief knock me over. "What did you want to talk about?"

"The short version is we'd like to encourage you to finish your degree. The longer version is I've spoken with Carter McKay, who I know is a family friend of yours, and he's unofficially warned me you might be considering holding out until August and going as a free agent. We don't want to see that happen."

Fucking Carter. I'd have to buy him a steak dinner for this. I checked the time on my phone. Eva had been waiting for over thirty minutes. She'd understand if I was late, but Archer was willing to set up another time. I might as well set my boundaries now.

"My girlfriend's expecting me, but I'm free after morning skate tomorrow. Why don't I meet you here?"

He grinned. "I heard you're dating Eva Adams. That girl is a handful, but she's solid gold."

Holy fuck, did *everyone* love Eva? The shock must have shown on my face because he clapped my shoulder. "It's a smaller world than you might think. I'll see you here tomorrow."

Archer walked away, and I stood rooted to the spot. My mind whirled with possibilities about Dallas, but I put it aside until later. Tonight was about Eva, and she was waiting.

A few people still lingered around the player exit, but I only saw the tiny blonde with the big attitude. She jumped at me, and I caught her easily. Her arms wound around my neck, and I kissed her, wild and raw, in front of anyone who wanted to see. Eva made a happy noise in her throat and eased back with a grin.

"You like my outfit?"

The material bunched under my hands, and I couldn't believe she'd pulled off that particular surprise. "Where did you find a jersey?"

"I bought it off a girl two rows back. Might as well make Dad's money useful one more time. I'm so proud of you. Did you talk to Archer?"

I gave her ass a light smack, since I could. "When were you going to tell me you knew Archer Bolme?"

A gleam of amusement lit her eyes. "It's complicated.

He's sort of dating my friend's mom, who I might have helped recently become single. I'm rooting for him."

"He wants to talk tomorrow—to make sure Dallas is my future."

She squealed and bounced a little, waking up my dick despite the very public setting. "I'm glad you got to play. Are you ready to go home? I have *plans* for you."

I chuckled and ran my nose along hers. "Because you love me."

Eva's smile softened. "Because I love you." Her voice lowered to a husky rasp. "And because I've been fantasizing about ripping that tux off you since you showed up earlier."

I'd never get enough of her. Her sassy mouth and her big heart and her ice blue eyes when she looked at me as if I was her entire world. Like she was mine.

"Fair enough." I allowed. "But first I'm diving under this skirt until you're coming on my tongue. Then I'm fucking you in my jersey."

She wiggled closer, sending a bolt of heat up my spine. "I should have known you'd love your name across my back."

"I love *you*, Eva Adams, no matter what you wear," I leaned down to growl into her ear. "But keep the tiara on."

EPILOGUE

Gavin

Several months later...

"I'm just saying Operation Naked Hockey Ass would work better if you spent more time outside of Gavin's room."

Eva snorted from the bed next to me, finishing up her Tuesday FaceTime with Stephen. "Pass. I have plenty of naked hockey ass right here." She shifted the camera toward me, splayed out on top of the tousled sheets, naked.

I glared at her, but she only stuck out her tongue.

Stephen shrieked from the other side of the call. "Wrong ass. Stop taunting me with your perfect boyfriend and get me illicit pics of Reece in a towel. Or not illicit. Better if he knows about them."

I turned my face into my pillow to hide my laugh. Reece would one hundred percent pose naked for pics. He wouldn't care who they were for, but he liked Stephen. Not in a romantic way, we'd discovered, but the two had hit it off. Stephen lived for flirting with Reece, who took it as his due.

"I'm not taking naked pictures of Reece, no matter how much he'd enjoy me asking."

"Sweet cheeks, we've talked about this. You have to use your unique position to the advantage of all mankind. The world deserves those pictures, and you continue to deny us." He shook his head sadly. "Thank god you're pretty."

Eva flipped him off with a sweet smile. "Oops, gotta go. *So* much dirty sex to have with my perfect boyfriend."

"Do good things," Stephen said with a laugh.

"And don't take shit from anyone." Eva made a kissy face at the camera then set her phone on the nightstand.

Henry quacked from the nest she'd made out of my shirt on the floor, and Eva sighed. "Okay, you can play with Cole, but come right back if he has company."

She climbed off the bed to open the door for the duck, who fluffed her feathers and waddled across the hall. I rolled over to watch the madness and shook my head. "I used to be the favorite."

"You're still my favorite." Eva checked to make sure Cole let her in before coming back to bed.

"I love Henry, but you have to admit it's weird the way you understand her."

She traced the dark outline of the flower tattoos on my arm. "My relationship with Henry is no weirder than your relationship with Danny. I can't believe he goes out and gets the same tattoos as you."

"Not the same. Variations on a theme. His flowers are different." I watched her face as she explored, waiting.

"Why flowers?"

"Mom loved to garden. She always had pots of growing things on every windowsill. The flowers are for her." The memory didn't hit as hard as it used to when I'd tried not to think about them. Eva encouraged me to tell her stories so she could get to know them too, and I was glad for the excuse to remember the good times.

Her finger moved up farther to the stylized wings. "And these?"

"My position. Right wing." I threw my arm across her middle, caressing the warm skin under the oversized shirt she was wearing.

She smiled at the roman numerals for fourteen, stroking the stark lines on my shoulder blade. "Your jersey number."

Her hand stilled on the fresh tattoo along my ribs—the one I'd gotten when she'd been out of town for a competition. "Gavin?"

"Yeah, it's for you." The tiara was simple and followed the curves of the other tattoos on my side.

"I thought we weren't hiding things anymore?" Her gaze locked on mine, suspiciously shiny.

"I wanted to surprise you. Not the same."

"You're really taking that perfect boyfriend title to heart." Her cheeks puffed out as she exhaled. "In the interest of not hiding things, I had a job interview today."

I stroked her side, noting the goosebumps rising where I touched. "Finally decided to end my misery and become a chef?"

She poked my back. "No, ass, at a cheer training facility in Dallas. They heard about the work I did with Delacourt and want to hire me in the same capacity."

"Is this job going to make you happy?"

"Yeah, I think it will. I'd be working part time, mostly remote, until I graduate."

I turned my head to kiss her hip. "I guess it's a good thing you'll be moving to Dallas after graduation then."

"I will?" The teasing in her voice turned into a sharp intake when I yanked the shirt over her head.

"I'll be training with the team, so I won't have a lot of time for cooking or cleaning. I could use someone…"

She threw an elbow, but I caught her arm and dragged her underneath me.

"Dallas is a good fit. I like Archer and their commitment to their players, but my number one priority is you. Which means you'll just have to come with me. Carter sent over some apartments for us to look at—"

Eva didn't let me finish. She pulled my head down for a scorching kiss.

"I'm glad you have a plan because you're not going without me. I can't help pay for it, not for a little while at least, but—"

I cut her off like she'd done with me. "I don't need your money. I have enough saved to cover until the season starts."

She frowned. "I hate feeling like I'm not contributing."

"I love you, and whatever our life looks like in Dallas, I'll love that too. You don't have to contribute, you only have to love me back. Trust me to take care of us."

Eva met my eyes, fire buried under the ice. "Done. Loving you is the easy part."

"Good girl," I murmured, skimming her jawline with my thumb. "Now spread your legs, Princess."

Get a glimpse of Gavin and Eva's happy ever after with the exclusive bonus epilogue.

Click here for your free bonus epilogue!

**If you're having trouble clicking, go to http://www.nikkihallbooks.com/ice-cold-player **

———

Want more of the Teagan University Wildcats?

Turn the page to see what happens when Cole has to be tutored by Avery, his coach's daughter, in Ice Cold Heart, the second book in the Beyond the Ice hockey romance series.

ICE COLD HEART

Cole

Red lipstick. I stared down at my book, not seeing the words past the memory of scarlet lips on a fuck you face. The same problem I'd been having since I'd seen her weeks ago—a beautiful moment of calm in the chaos of the team's celebration. Hockey players weren't subtle about our wins, and she'd walked right through all of us to talk to Coach as if we weren't there.

Lucky bastard.

I scrubbed a hand down my face and pushed the book away. Might as well take a break since none of the words were registering anyway. My fingers tapped out a random rhythm on the scarred table as I let the visual play out. I'd only caught a glimpse of the girl, less than a minute before she'd disappeared down the tunnel on her heeled boots.

Oh yeah, I'd committed her to memory. Tight jeans cupping a full ass, hips swaying, long dark hair brushing her back. My dick perked up at the image, and I sighed. She might as well have stepped out of my dreams. Even if she hadn't sported an invisible do not touch sign, even if she hadn't spoken *only* to Coach, I doubted I'd ever see her again. What were the chances?

I leaned back in the uncomfortable padded chair, wincing at the pain in my lower back and wishing the school wasn't so stingy. Teagan University was an expensive private university boasting some of the best sports teams in college athletics, but they sucked at providing for the average students. A rich alumnus had donated enough to build a state-of-the-art hockey arena, which resulted in TU developing a DI hockey team on the way to the Frozen Four.

And the chairs in the library had to be at least twenty years old.

I stretched my arms over my head, twisting to pop my back, and surveyed the crowded room. Finals week was the worst time to find a quiet spot in the library. Every table was full of students with crazed eyes quizzing each other. Loudly. I'd carved out a space on the second floor, but my small table was at the edge of the main study area.

My gaze snagged on a girl sitting alone several tables down, nearly hidden in the corner. The fall of her straight dark hair blocked most of her face, but I caught a hint of red lipstick. And I'd recognize those boots anywhere.

No fucking way.

I blinked a couple of times, half expecting my dream girl to disappear, but she tilted her head back to take a sip from the disposable coffee cup next to her. My heart raced at the sight of the girl I couldn't get out of my mind. Sheer disbelief rooted me to my chair. TU had to have something like ten thousand students, and luck had shined down on me.

If my roommate, Reece, hadn't been blasting his music like a dumbass, I wouldn't have ventured out to the library and found her again. I could never tell him that. His ego would become unwieldy, and we'd have to shave his head like we'd done to Jaden after the naked footrace incident.

Before I could figure out a way to go over there without looking like a stalker, another guy approached her table. Medium height and build, no backpack, cocky smile—he wasn't looking for somewhere to study. I crossed my arms and tried not to glare in their direction.

The guy tried to pull the chair next to her out, but she caught it with her leg, preventing it from going anywhere. She didn't even look up from the textbook in front of her.

Despite the volume level, I could hear her clearly. "Nope."

He leaned down into her face to say something I didn't catch, and I almost shot from my seat. Slowly, her eyes rose, green and gorgeous and full of disdain. Her red lips moved, quietly, and the guy jerked back like she'd slapped him.

Apparently, she didn't need my help after all. A quick shot of pride had me settling back into my chair.

With a bored look, she gathered her books and drink, then slung her bag over her shoulder. The guy smirked at her and moved in again. I had a brief moment of insanity where I considered tossing the asshole off the balcony in the middle of the room. If I could slam guys twice his size into the glass, I could definitely heft him.

Dream Girl turned on her heel and walked away, completely ignoring him. Instead of following her, he sat down at her table, forcing me to abandon my plan. Attempted murder probably wasn't the best way to get her attention. I surreptitiously watched her leave, wishing I'd taken the time to look around the room earlier. The urge to chase after her was strong, but she'd already been accosted once today. I didn't like my chances.

Besides, I'd caught a glimpse of the logo on her coffee

cup. Market Street Coffee. I knew the place. Hell, our house was only a couple of blocks from there.

Dream Girl wasn't entirely a mystery anymore. She was a student, she knew Coach, and she went to Market Street for her coffee. I'd see her again—if I could ever get through the damn book for my upcoming English class.

I unclenched from the encounter I hadn't even been a part of and picked up the offending text. Most of the students around me were focused on their finals, but I'd already finished mine. My stress stemmed from my schedule for next semester and the last required course for my junior year—English lit.

Whoever had decided a psychology degree needed an extra English class could kiss my ass. I'd dropped twice already, and this was my last chance according to the university's rules. The degree wasn't necessary to play professional hockey—I'd already been drafted by Denver—but I'd promised my parents I'd finish school. And I'd promised myself I'd help our team win the Frozen Four.

All I had to do was pass one damn class. The rest was easy.

A giggle interrupted my musing, and I made the mistake of absently glancing toward a group of girls two tables over. They smiled at me, and I recognized their predatory expressions. Puck bunnies in disguise.

I didn't hate the attention. Most of the girls I met were nice once they realized I had no interest in a hookup. But today wasn't a good day. We had two and a half weeks off, then my hockey schedule was going to explode. At my best, I was a slow reader. With practice and games and other classes... and the occasional duck-sitting, I didn't have time to read slow.

Frustration threatened to choke me when I thought

about possibly failing and losing my scholarship and my chance to play at TU. Prepping for next semester needed to come before everything else. I couldn't bring myself to be a dick to the girls, so I picked up the book, hoping they'd take the hint and leave me be.

A subtly sweet scent hit me seconds before the chair next to mine scraped out on the industrial tile. My gaze snapped up, and I saw red, red lips before meeting a pair of vibrant green eyes fringed by thick lashes.

Dream Girl winked and sat down as if she belonged there, our legs nearly touching. Behind her, I saw one of the puck bunnies resume her seat with a pinched expression. Clearly, the hint wasn't going to work if she'd already been on her way over.

"Sorry I'm late, I didn't see you over here," Dream Girl said loudly enough to carry to all the tables.

Amusement—and pure lust—had me smiling at the game she was playing. "I'd wait for you all day..." I trailed off, hoping she'd fill in her name.

"Avery," she whispered, leaning in close.

"Cole," I responded in the same hushed tone.

We didn't move for a long moment with our eyes locked and a secret passing between us. I told myself to say something, but her nearness short-circuited my brain making me blurt out the first question that crossed my mind.

"What are you doing?"

Avery laughed. "Giving them a reason not to come over here. You have to help me sell it though. Talk to me like you're fascinated by me. Tell me what you're doing over the break."

I snorted, struggling to get a handle on my racing heart. "Probably reading."

She tilted her head. "What did the poor books do to you?"

"I'm sure they're fine." I lied, and the truth spilled out of me. "I was supposed to go home to my grandpa's farm, but I have too many responsibilities here."

Her brows shot up. "A farm boy, huh? You look the part. Broad shoulders and all those muscles. You should really get into sports."

There was a small chance she didn't know I was a starter on the TU hockey team, but if she knew Coach, I doubted it. Still, I didn't like beginning with a lie. I tried to work out a way to tell her I was a star hockey player without sounding like a jackass, but the words wouldn't come. Luckily, Avery saved me the trouble.

She leaned in to pat my cheek. "I'm fucking with you. I know who you are."

I caught her wrist before she could pull away, and my thumb picked up her rapid pulse. Maybe I wasn't the only one affected. She tugged gently, and I released her.

"Why are you helping me?" I asked.

Avery shrugged. "You looked ready to defend my honor earlier. I thought I'd return the favor."

"You noticed me?"

She chuckled. "You're hard to miss, farm boy. Half the women in here are salivating over you while glaring at me. If looks could kill, I'd be dead on the floor from your fan club over there."

A loud thud came from the puck bunny table, followed by a snicker and a whistle from behind me.

"Don't look their way," she warned.

"No chance." I couldn't wrench my attention away from Avery even if I'd wanted to. As far as I was concerned, we were alone in the library.

Avery's hair brushed my skin when she turned her head to study my expression. At some point, I'd stretched my arm across the back of her chair. Not exactly smooth, but she hadn't drawn away. Something must have passed muster because the tension she'd been carrying since I spotted her relaxed. Her shoulders dropped, and she shifted closer to me.

Only inches separated her pretty face from mine. The air between us heated, and I tried not to groan when she wet her lips. I *would not* hit on her while she was trying to help me. My dick didn't get the message, and I hoped she wouldn't glance down any time soon.

Avery reached out for the book I'd forgotten, examining it as she turned it over in her hands. "Is it always like this when you're trying to study?"

"It's a real problem," I murmured.

She set the book down carefully, and a slow grin curled her lips. "Well then, let's give them a reason to stay away."

My breath caught at the mischief in her green eyes as she quirked an eyebrow for permission. I dropped my chin in a tiny nod, praying she'd do something crazy like climb into my lap right there in the study area.

As if she could hear my thoughts, the girl of my dreams closed the distance and pressed her red lips against mine.

A NOTE FROM NIKKI

Thank you so much for reading Ice Cold Player! I've been wanting to write Eva's book from the moment she appeared at lunch in Game Changer. The second Gavin showed up and denied her free espresso in Rule Breaker, I knew he'd be the man for her. I had so much fun exploring their explosive chemistry, and their backstories hit me right in the feels. I hope you enjoyed reading the book as much as I enjoyed writing it.

This isn't the end for Eva, since you'll see her in Cole's book, up next, and where Eva goes, Gavin goes. Though honestly, you'll probably see more of Henry than either of them. No regrets. Henry deserves her own fan club.

If you have a second, please consider leaving a review. Even better, tag me with the review so we can be besties. You can find me on Facebook, Instagram, or TikTok. Finally, if you want updates on future books and other fun stuff, join my newsletter. I promise not to bite.

ACKNOWLEDGMENTS

I'd like to thank (in no particular order):

- Nicole Schneider, Liz Gallegos, and Megan Clements, for making the words go in a pleasing manner
- Santiago's, the carnitas and bean burrito fueled me through many a writing sprint
- Angela Haddon, your covers give me life
- Romance Writers of the Rockies, for accepting me as I am
- The Tuesday Writing Girlies, I'm going to need several more happy hours
- The Hubs, I wouldn't want to do this life with anyone else
- Cold brew with almond milk and coconut syrup, coffee is basically water, right?
- Skadior on Instagram, your character art is BEAUTIFUL
- My readers, your hair looks great today

ALSO BY NIKKI HALL

Wild Card series

Game Changer

Rule Breaker

Front Runner

Hard Hitter

Play Maker

Beyond the Ice series

Ice Cold Player

Ice Cold Heart

ABOUT THE AUTHOR

Nikki Hall is a smart-ass with a Ph.D. and a potty mouth. She writes happy ever after stories with found families, sassy heroines, and strong men who love their women hard. Coffee makes her happy, messes make her stabby, and she'd sell one of her children for a second season of Firefly.

Want to find out when the newest Nikki Hall book hits the shelves? Sign up for her newsletter at www.nikkihallbooks.com/signup.

Printed in Dunstable, United Kingdom